THE BLUE MAN
and other stories from Wales

The Blue Man
and other stories from Wales

chosen by

Christine Evans

First Impression—October 1995
Second Impression—June 1996

ISBN 1 85902 228 6

This book is published with the support of the Arts Council of Wales.

Printed in Wales at
Gomer Press, Llandysul, Dyfed

To the pupils at
Bryn Hafren and
Barry Boys' Comprehensive Schools,
Barry—with thanks.

Contents

Tadpoles

It was almost summer—May, I think, last year. The sheep had finished dropping their lambs and I had been helping Mum get the caravans ready for the visitors. It was also the summer Ali fell in love. It was funny watching her putting mascara on and shaving her armpits. Where she'd shaved it the skin was blue-white, just like the leathery skin of snakes' eggs in the biology books at school.

Mum said, 'Madonna never shaves her armpits.'

'Madonna's old,' said Ali, staring intensely at her chin for any sign of blackhead activity.

Mum gave up.

I was busy with the tadpoles I found in the boggy field by the river. It's good down there. Sometimes there's mushroom rings and you can stand in the middle and make wishes and that. I found loads of it, frogspawn, I mean, but only about six had made it to tadpoles, and two already had their back legs.

The tadpoles were tiny, wet and glistening like black, shiny jewels. Ali hated them.

'Slimy things!' she'd hiss, wafting down the stairs in a cloud of 'Irresistible' body spray. 'Do you have to have them in our room?' she'd yell, 'Their water stinks!'

For years before that, Ali had come with me to

look for frogspawn. We were never close like some sisters —she was always that bit older—but we used to like the same things. I mean, I wouldn't have got into all this eco-stuff if it wasn't for her. I used to think nature was a series on BBC2 with David Attenborough, and recycling was blowing your nose twice on the same tissue.

But then she just got too busy for anything, anything that didn't have Geraint in it. Geraint was the boyfriend. I call him 'Granite' because he's craggy and dense.

That summer Geraint was always lurking in the front room smiling at Mum and Dad, and every time, not just the once or twice, but every time, he'd say 'Hiya Squirt!' to me, like it was funny.

I told you he was dense.

After I got upset I just got used to it. Got used to my sister turning into someone else, someone I didn't know. Someone who started eating meat again because Granite did, someone who started wearing nail varnish seriously, and having baths that took nearly an hour.

Mum and Dad thought it was perfectly normal. In fact they seemed pleased, especially Dad. I heard him:

'Well, love, what did I say! I knew she'd grow out of it all, all that "green" stuff. That boy's the world of good for Ali!'

Mum just hmmed. I could tell she was less enthusiastic, but I didn't hear any more because of the noise of the washing up.

It was only a few weeks after Easter, but it was hot already, and sitting on the school bus at the end of the day all smelly and sweaty was the worst. The windows all seemed to be jammed shut and it felt as though the journey took longer every day. The bus always stopped for me and Ali just on the far side of the village, in a layby that used to be a bend in the road.

Anyway, the bus pulled over, engine throbbing, belching out grey thick bus exhaust, only it didn't pull right over, it couldn't. The layby was full of caravans. Not like the two shiny new caravans we keep in the top field for visitors, not like that. These caravans were bigger, shiny, yes, the windows filled with lacy satin curtains. There was a truck, and a couple of little kids grubbing about in the dirt with toys, like kids do. There were shiny silver billycans like milk churns and the hedge was strewn with drying clothes. Pink and white, knickers and bras, Wrestling T-shirts and shiny track suit bottoms. Funny flowers.

All the kids on the bus were gawping, mouths open gawping. There was a fat woman spreading out the clothes, and she stared right back. I heard someone mutter 'Gypsies!'

Ali grabbed me—'Come on!' and pulled me out of the bus and through the camp round to our gate. I knew I was gawping too, and I couldn't help it. Gypsies, these were really gypsies. But they didn't have painted caravans like in books, or horses or headscarves. A girl rounded a caravan and stepped out in front of us, almost blocking our way, right in front of our gate. I stared at her, right into her light blue eyes. She was holding a bundle of washing, almost snarling at us. Ali didn't look, she just opened the gate and walked straight up, as if they weren't there.

Mum had already phoned the council. Dad was furious. My tadpoles were flittering, unworried in their fishtank. I was thinking I'd wait till they were all froglets before I'd take them back. Our phone never stopped ringing. Some committee was being organised, meetings were planned. Granite was taking Ali to the cinema.

Not long after supper people started arriving. Mum said I could watch telly in her bedroom. I knew they wanted me out of the way. So I sat at the top of the stairs where I could listen and watch.

Ali had on this flowery, floppy, flouncy frock, her brown curly hair caught up loosely at the back of her head. She looked like a Spanish dancer. Or a gypsy. She stared at her reflection in the landing

12

mirror, teasing bits of hair out—'the tousled look' it's called in those mags—then pursing her lips up and smearing them with coloured whale blubber. (OK, so I'm going over the top a bit there).

She smacked her lips, blotted them with tissue and smiled at me.

'How do I look?'

I opened my mouth to say something witty and cutting, but she was gone. I hung over the top of the bannister like I used to when I was little.

'Gone with the Raggle Taggle Gypsies O!' I sang.

Dad glared at me. 'Hannah! Go and watch telly!'

That was when I knew it was really serious.

I ended up in our room, watching the tadpoles.

I try and imagine growing legs. Is it like bursting? Or pressure, pressure forcing outwards into leg-shapes, arm-shapes. Webbed hand shapes. How does it feel?

Out of the window the daylight had just gone. I could see the grey sea in the distance, and the lights of the caravans. Not camp fires and tambourines, but that blue-white telly light. Just like everyone else.

I wondered if Ali and Granite were kissing.

Snogging. Smearing the greasy red all round her mouth.

Downstairs they were talking about rubbish. Smells. Stealing. Putting off the visitors. Children not going to school. Running wild. More stealing.

The people downstairs weren't strangers. There was Mrs. Robinson who runs the paper shop, the new woman from the Pub, Mr. Williams at the Garage and the people who have the next farm along, Jean and Ted they're called. They sounded so different now, so fiery. I looked over at the caravans. There was no violin or guitar music, no saucy dancing by the campfire. What looked like the fat woman was shuffling along the hedge, picking off the clothes.

I felt like I didn't know them at all, those grown-ups downstairs. Even now, all this time later when Mrs. Robinson smiles at me I still think of all that hate inside, and I'm scared. Really scared. Scared in case I've got hate like that in me. It was different from hating Lowri Turner at school—a different, bigger, frightening hate.

The gypsies went after two weeks and Dad had a barbecue to celebrate. I was glad too. It felt like walking through someone's sitting room, just going into the village. Why couldn't they be somewhere else? And then I'd feel guilty, and I was sure they could tell what you were thinking just by looking at you.

The day after the barbecue Granite chucked Ali. I was glad, but made the mistake of saying so.

'I hate you Hannah, you're poisonous!' Ali yelled, and stormed out crying. I saw her run off up the mountain and I was going to go after her, but ended up wandering round where the gypsies had been instead.

It did smell funny, sort of disinfectanty, mixed with an old musty clothes smell. You could see where the caravans had been and there was a pile of rubbish buzzing with flies. I wondered where they'd gone.

I tried being nice to Ali, I really did try. But it was no use. She was still different, even without Granite. My Ali had gone.

Tomorrow, I thought, I'm going to set the froglets free.

Catherine Johnson

Boy of Dreams

'Settle down, you lot!' Old Barney raised his cracked voice with an effort, as if he were tired. 'I have an announcement . . .'

Cefin studied the drab teacher; crumpled suit, lined face. Did Old Barney worry about gas and electricity bills? Cefin's parents worried a lot about those sort of things. They quarrelled over money and never knew where it went. Perhaps, in a secret place, there was a huge mountain made of money—(unlike Cefin's Dad)—and everybody's wages ended up on this mountain, the silver and gold growing higher and higher . . . with slaves shovelling on the coins stolen from millions of Mams and Dads and Old Barneys . . .

'Cefin Lewis! Are you with us?'

'Yes, Mr Barnes.' A narrow squeak, that. Old Barney hated dreamers. He liked concentration— 'Think about what you are doing! Train your minds not to wander!'

Cefin's mind was the worst in the class for wandering. It was untrainable, like a bad dog. Off it would go of its own accord, out of the window, miles away . . .

'So, as I was saying, if any boy or girl wishes to take part then let me have letters from home. Saturdays and Sundays only in term-time. Every day in the holidays. When the replies are sorted out, we'll organise a rota. Got all that?'

Cefin had got very little. Take part in *what*? Take turns doing *what*?

The corridor bell shrilled, chairs shot back and clanked against each other and voices gabbled. Old Barney shouted but gave up, defeated by the din. School was over and Cefin no wiser.

But Cefin had worked out a method for catching up on anything he missed. He never admitted to dreaming and not listening but drew out the information, word by word, on his walks home with Evan and Arwel.

'What about Old Barney's idea, then?'

'Not *his* idea, is it?' They thought it up on the Council. Then some companies got interested.' Arwel knew everything.

'Well—yes—I know that.' Cefin put on a confident swagger to hide his ignorance. He knew nothing whatsoever about the Council or companies. Try again. 'But Old Barney's asking for the letters about us—um—taking part.'

'I don't want to,' Evan said, deftly kicking a can. 'There's football and swimming. I won't have time.' Arwel tipped the can in a low arc back to Evan. This was no good. In two seconds they'd be absorbed in their footwork and talk would be finished.

'I'm going to take part!' There. Now they would have to say more about it. Whatever it was.

Evan whooped in horror. 'You'll have to dress up! Clogs and caps—all that creepy old stuff. Eeurgh!'

'I won't mind that.' Clogs? Caps? Something to do with the Eisteddfod? Nothing made sense yet. 'Erm—er—any idea what I'd have to do?'

Arwel shrugged. 'Just hang about—behaving like those old mouldies.'

'You might have to milk a cow or feed the pigs. Mucky things like that.' Evan relished this, well out of it.

The olden days. Cefin's bad-dog mind was on the leash. He held on tightly. Go carefully . . . 'Yes. I see. You mean—act like—like it was a hundred years ago.'

''Course. My Dad says the tourists will go for it. Trips down the Old Pit are okay but people want more. The whole way of life.'

The three boys came to the top of the footpath.

'See? They've finished mending the row of cottages. And the shop. Just like it used to be. My Dad says that to get it right they copied old photographs out of St Fagan's Museum.' The discussion in Arwel's house was wonderful.

A board stretched out between two posts

18

displayed lettering, black on white. SITE FOR CWMTRUAN THEME PARK. Cefin guessed the rest easily. And he liked it.

'Yeah! We dress up and show visitors how it was in the old days!'

Evan twisted an ugly face. 'Don't forget the pigs! You'll have to clean out the sty! *Ych a fi*!'

The strip of colliers' houses, like a long stone railway coach, was set on the brow of the hill. Proud now, with sturdy new doors and window-frames, tidy garden squares at the back and a well-made approach road. The sign GENERAL STORES hung, artfully crooked, over the doorway. Outside the shop, a man was hammering at a bench. All their lives, until recently, the boys had known these buildings as ruins; roofless, with under-nourished grass and weeds desperate against the disintegrating walls; a place to play hide-and-seek and dares.

'My Dad says they can't make it like it used to be,' said Evan. His Dad's favourite phrase was 'what's the use?'

'Near enough,' said Arwel, whose Dad believed in progress.

Cefin wondered what it was like, long ago, living in one of these cottages, little and cramped, with a view of the mineshaft winding-gear below and the cruel wind whipping off the hill. Not so good, he imagined. Still, pretending would be painless . . .

'You're not getting involved in that Theme Park!' Cefin's Dad was (1) dead against the whole idea, (2) ashamed of the Council and (3) fearful for the reputation of Wales.

'Don't be daft,' said Cefin's Mam. 'It's living history.'

'It's Disneyland with Welshcakes,' scorned Dad. 'What's the country coming to? Where's the dignity in it? Have they no pride?'

'Don't be such a misery!' Mam gave Dad a superior look of contempt. 'You're always moaning about Cef stuck in front of the television. Now he wants to get out, you won't let him!' Her voice softened as she turned to Cefin. 'Don't worry, my lovely. I'll write the letter for you.'

'Gurr . . .!' Dad said things like that when he was lost for words. 'Have it your own way, then.' He subsided into a kind of sulk grumble. 'I'm going over to see our Delwyn. I bet his kids won't be making fools of themselves at the Theme Park!'

'Where's your community spirit?' shouted Mam after him, laughing. Cefin could rely on her for that. She always finished up in good humour.

The boy on the low wooden stool huddled towards

the fire, smokey and acrid in the iron basket-grate. He fisted his cold fingers, folding them under the sleeves of his rough flannel shirt. The old man, nearly sightless, gazed from the corner settle.

'Out with you, *'ngwas i*! Fresh air in your lungs, you need.'

'All right, Gransha.'

He was glad to obey. It was warmer outside than in the dark little kitchen. His mother, stout and breathless, was struggling to hang heavy washing on a line in the unmade yard. Her hair— still nut-brown in spite of everything—dropped from its pins and her feet in the cracked boots trod painfully on the stony ground. The wooden tub slopped with more soaking linen, the mis-shapen lump of soap hard as month-old cheese on the ridged wash-board.

'Shall I help you, Mam?'

'I can manage—this is no work for a boy.' Her red hands pushed the whittled gypsy pegs over the heavy wet clothes, squeezing them fast onto the line. 'Where are you off to? Mischief, is it?'

'No, Mam. I'll walk over to see Aunty Beccy, if you like.'

'No, you won't! You stay away from there— she'll think that I sent you on purpose—that I don't feed you.'

The boy was always hungry, it was true. And

Aunty Beccy spoiled him with *teisen lap* and creamy milk.

'I'll go *tro i fyny*, then.'

His mother spoke in one unbroken string of commands and queries, without pausing. 'Mind you do, *'te*—don't go down *dacw* fighting with those Donovan boys—d'you hear me?—and where's your coat?'

He was third or fourth owner of the old brown jacket but it was snug enough over the rough shirt and knee-breeches. His mother had unpicked the lining and padded it out with layers of newspaper for extra warmth.

He was off now and away. Out into the luring sunshine, weak as yet but promising to lift the chill out of him once he started walking. He had this first of the year excitement in him—and he would always have that, free of charge.

A girl came out of a house further down the row. 'Hey!' she called and came closer. Her boldness more than made up for her shabby, drooping skirt and old woman's shawl. 'You going out, then? I'll come with you.'

'Nobody asked you,' said the boy without halting. The sun was momentarily masked by a small cloud. He walked on, his back rejecting her. She caught up with him and walked in step, not caring that she wasn't wanted. He tried not to look at her long braided hair and her sideways smile.

'Our mam is having another baby. That's seven,' she said.

The boy didn't know how she put up with so many infants bawling and screaming in a house only two up, two down. He lived only with Mam, Da and Gransha, *diolch i Dduw*. He shared a room with his grandfather but had a bed all to himself.

'I might go to London,' the girl said. She arched her eyebrows and pulled back her shoulders, fancying her chances. 'Go into service. I'm nearly old enough.'

'Go, then.' His sisters were in service. They had awful tales to tell of flights of stairs and back-breaking coal scuttles, blacklead and brass polish. She'd find out.

Getting no response, she quickly forgot her ambitions. 'Where we goin' now, then?' She was all skippy and silly as if he'd planned an outing especially for her.

He tramped on, not answering. He rested only once in his climb to look at the knot of dwellings and the pithead below in the bowl of the valley. His father was beneath the scene, deep down in the darkness. He shook away the thought and went on again. He turned upwards, going over the hill, the girl following, determined. They walked on until the land was foreign and they bent under ancient, stunted shapes which had once striven to be apple trees.

'The weather's on the turn now!' He wished she'd stop her senseless prattle. He could just hear a blackbird in the distance and he wanted to listen, fill himself with the glorious song set in the wide, empty sky.

The boy came to a stone wall, strongly built and patchy with encroaching lichen and black-green ivy.

'Hey! You can't go in there!'

'Who says?'

The boy jumped onto the wall, hoping the barrier would rid him of his uninvited companion.

'Wait for me!'

He sighed, hope going. Then he jumped down into forbidden ground. Before straightening up, he looked about him, wary, alert. Stillness. The bird called a pure, clear welcome.

But the girl followed, landing heavily without his help, giving a little shocked shriek and a giggle.

'Quiet, can't you?' He wanted to savour the air, magically sweet in this loamy warmth which he had no right to walk in. But he walked on, now softly on mats of dead leaves, now crisply on a litter of twigs, tense with courage and curiosity. He listened—but the bird sang no more.

They walked along the faint winding trail, dipping beneath low-growling canopies and stamping down brambles. The girl kept close to him, and her chatter ceased. As they moved on, they hardly noticed the subtle changes all around them, nor the appearance of carefully cultivated plants. They were on dangerous ground.

Suddenly, another voice fluted through the stillness, echoing against the slope of the ground.

'Stop! You are trespassing!'

In the branches of a young tree they saw a boy of their own age. He wore a knickerbocker suit of fine tweed, crowned with a velvet cap. He looked down, disdain on his thin curved lips.

'*Pwy wyt ti?*' the boy on the ground wanted to know. No harm in asking.

The boy above folded his arms and his voice came out with a bit of arrogance.

'I forbid you to speak in your barbarian language!'

The boy's knowing brown eyes hardened. 'Then we will speak in *your* barbarian language— all right?'

'How dare you? I'll call my father's bailiff. He'll deal with you.'

'Oh—Old Jenkins. Proper lackey, he is. Can't you fight your own battles, like a man?'

The girl pulled at the threadbare jacket. 'Come *on*,' she urged, hush-voiced with fear. 'He can make trouble. Put our fathers out of work if he likes.'

The boy knew the wisdom of this but his teeth were set firm and his hands clenched, burning now, not cold.

'We lost our way,' spoke up the girl. She was quick with her wits, *'ware teg.* 'We don't mean any harm.'

The other boy's saxe-blue glare despised them. Behind him, seen through the groomed parkland in the far-off early spring mist, the big house was an impression, unnoticed as if in the background of a pale picture.

'Your father's in there, is he?'

'We don't want any unpleasantness,' said the girl, haughty as London. 'We are leaving at once.'

Her straight look warned the boys and said, more strongly than words— 'No sense—you boys. Always ready for a fight when most things can be got round with a bit of tact.' She caught at his sleeve to turn him away. And he almost went.

'Peasants!' spat the other boy. 'Thieves!'

That did it.

Straight out with the boy's right arm, the compacted knuckles cracking into the fine bone of the tormentor's jaw. His stringy body lunged forward, arms attacking, defending, pulling, pushing. He caught handfuls of warm tweed and felt his old coat give way and tear. The velvet cap toppled, trampled by the four pounding feet and the girl screamed. A dog barked in the nearby gardens, a man shouted and both came running.

'What's all this? *Down* Caesar! Are you all right, Master Cedric?' Glossy blood wormed thickly from the trembling mouth. The dog growled suspiciously at the intruders, knowing his work and cheated of it. The man looked at the damaged lip and advised the injured boy to go back to the house. Silently, servant and master conspired. A man's fight was his own affair. Nothing would be said, no recriminations, no loss of face. Badly shaken, Master Cedric stumbled away towards the even lawns.

The bailiff turned to the others. 'I haven't seen you two ruffians. Not this time. Make sure there is no next time. Now get along home with you.'

'You should have come away when I said,' the girl complained when they were over the wall again. 'You know his sort. Little lord of the manor. We can't win.'

Still, the boy felt that he had won something, although exactly what it was escaped him. He was also hungry. Fights and arguments were all right in their place but dinner was best. There was *cawl* in the big pot, ready by now.

When he went into the kitchen, his Uncle

Howells was there. Mam was tidy and serene in a clean pinafore and Gransha smiled, seeing nothing but cheered by the visitor and the smell of the simmering soup.

Red-necked and pleased with himself, Uncle Howells wore a brown suit, rigid paper collar and an important bowler hat.

'Look at the state of you, *twpsyn*! Been through a hedge backwards! Smarten up a bit!' At his mother's fussing, the boy held his coat around him, clutching at the scraps of paper which surfaced through the cloth.

Uncle Howells did not mind what he looked like. Cherry-faced, he beamed his blessing on the boy. 'Good news, *bach*! Down the pit for you on Monday. I've got a start for you at last. Come along with your Da! What d'you say to that, now?'

The boy stared at his toe-caps.

'Cat got your tongue? Big boy like you—thank Uncle Howells nice, now.'

The boy lifted his head slowly to face them. Understanding very little, they thought that his eyes were filled with tears of gratitude.

'What's wrong with the boy, then?'

'He might be going down with 'flu. Moping about the place. Not even got the telly on.'

Cefin could hear them, not bickering but united in their concern for him.

'Hi, our Cef. Not so good, then?'

Dad came in and sat down in a dralon armchair. He turned up the blaze of the mock-log gas fire.

'I'm okay, Dad.'

Cefin had not changed out of the costume (run up by his Mam on her Swiss electronic sewing machine) which he wore for his Theme Park job. He longed for his jeans and T-shirt but the old-style clothes seemed to press on him, reluctant to let him go.

'Have a nice bath. A good old soak, right? Get into your jammies and dressing gown. It's my turn to get the tea. Fishburgers! You like them, Cef.'

Dad was doing his best. For all his bluster what he cared for most was Mam and Cefin and making them happy.

'Dad. I think I need to talk to you.'

Dad held his breath. Then — 'Oh, er—better see your mother. She knows all about—'

'Dad. Stay just a minute.'

Dad crouched back into the chair, trying to smile as he waited.

Cefin had no pattern to follow for this. He'd probably be told not to be dull. He gave his speech a trial run in his head.

29

'Dad—do you think we can remember things from the past? Long ago?'

Dad would lean forward. 'Oh, yes. Definitely. The day my brother Delwyn was born—I remember it like it was yesterday. Somebody said something stupid — "Your nose will be cut out now!" I was scared for years—thought they were going to cut off my nose!'

'No, Dad. Not those sort of memories. I mean —days before we were born. Things about—people who lived before.'

Dad would be uneasy with this. His world was firmly fenced with practical matters.

'What—um—what exactly are you saying, Cef?'

Cefin would launch into it then. 'It was slow at the Theme Park today. Hardly any visitors. It was okay for a whole. I read a book and talked to Mrs Bowen. Then I sat by the fire. And—suddenly—I was somebody else. Long ago.'

Dad would make that jokey frown of his. 'You dropped off to sleep, Cef! A vivid dream, it was. And no wonder! The whole place here is Theme Park crazy!'

That's how it would be. He'd never be believed about the people he had lived with on that bright spring day and the blackbird singing its heart out.

Thinking that his Dad had actually spoken,

Cefin said quietly, 'Yes, Dad. That was it. You're right.' He stood up. 'I'll go and have my bath now. Can I watch television while I'm eating?'

Dad, more confused than ever, was glad to be let off the hook. 'Why not? Hurry up then. The famous Cwmtruan chef is about to swing into action!'

'Yes, Dad. That was it.'

But it wasn't. He thought of the strange old clothes, wearing them again in his imagination. Harsh, uncomfortable, not the smooth fit of Mam's version. He closed his eyes and swayed slightly. The tearing sound of worn-out fabric . . . the old jacket padded with news sheets . ...

'You all right, Cef?'

Cefin steadied himself, felt awkward, having nothing to say.

'Oh—I think I'll give up the Theme Park.'

'Good lad! I knew you'd see reason. Get out and play football with the lads. Best news I've heard all day!' Relief lit up Dad's face. 'Is that all that's on your mind?'

Not trusting himself to speak, Cefin nodded. Dad jumped up, pleased, and went to start his job at the microwave.

'He's overtired,' Cefin heard him say.

'Nothing to worry about. He's packing in his career with that three-ring circus!' Then Dad started singing 'O Sole Mio' to the fishburgers.

The bath relaxed Cefin—there were oceans of hot water in their house. Dressed early in his night clothes and with so much fuss about his welfare going on downstairs, he had the good feeling of being petted and nursed without the nastiness of being ill.

'You're missing it!' Mam shouted, slamming the iron about on one of Dad's shirts. 'Your serial on the telly!'

Somehow, though, all that seemed not to matter. That was fiction. Never equal to the real thing. The Theme Park was fiction too, except in the middle of it somewhere lay the real thing.

Without hurry, Cefin opened his hand and saw the fragment he had kept for hours. All he needed to know. A yellowed corner of a newspaper with the date in precise, ornate print. For the year . . . 1891 . . .

Pamela Purnell

Mr. Beynon and the Vandal

A large orange leaf presses against the window like a giant hand. I look through its fingers to where empty crisp packets mingle with autumn leaves down in the playground. Beyond the playground is Mr Beynon, the Headmaster; he's watching the teachers' carpark through a pair of binoculars.

Inside, we're in English with Mrs Shearer. I'm by the window, watching the Headmaster and listening to the class. We've been reading this book about a nuclear attack and how this family's stuck in the living-room, waiting till it's safe to go out. They discover, too late, that dust has been falling down the chimney and into their drinking water.

'A little bit of dust never harms nobody,' says Emma Leyshon.

'It's not ordinary dust,' says Ceri Evans, 'it's nucular.'

'Wha?' says Emma.

'New—queue—lar dust,' says Ceri slowly.

'An' what's that when it's at home?' says Dai Rix.

'Dust outa the sky,' says Ceri. Under his school uniform, he's wearing a purple T-shirt with MUSCLEMAN printed on it in big yellow letters.

'Ordinary dust just falls down,' says Emma, like she really knows. She's swinging her feet back and forth, like she's a clock.

'And I suppose new-clear dust falls sideways, does it?' says Andrea.

Mr Beynon's binoculars are fixed on something in the carpark. I follow his gaze and see someone hiding among the cars. It's Rhodri Rhys, huddled inside his duffle coat watching autumn leaves riding the wind. I've been wondering what he's doing in the carpark. As I watch, I see Mr. Beynon tiptoeing across the yard, making straight for Rhodri. I try to warn him, but he won't look up. Suddenly Mr Beynon appears from behind a car, grabs Rhodri's hood and yanks him out of sight.

'The Headmaster's got Rhodri!' I tell Andrea, but she's not listening. She's chewing at her bottom lip, deep in her own thoughts. Been acting funny all week, has Andrea, and won't say why.

'Right,' says Mrs Shearer. 'Let's get down to work. I want you to design a poster to tell people what to do if there's a nuclear attack.' She goes on to say we have to write instructions like SEAL ALL DOORS AND WINDOWS and DO NOT PANIC, and draw pictures to illustrate them. 'Find a partner,' she says, 'and plan the poster between you.'

'My partner's not here,' says Dai. 'Where's Rhodri Rhys?'

'He was feeling sick,' says Mrs Shearer. 'I said

he could go out for some fresh air. He should be back any minute.'

'The Headmaster's got him,' I say, but no-one's listening; they're too busy finding partners and paper and tables to work on.

Andrea pairs up with Pietro, because he's the only one who can draw. Emma Leyshon picks me to share her 24 coloured pencils: six each of yellow, red, blue and green. While Dai's waiting for Rhodri he wanders from desk to desk, nicking things.

'What's that you've drawn?' he says, poking his fingers at our poster.

'What do you think it is, Dai?' says Emma, proudly.

'Looks like a tree,' he says, putting a blue in his pocket.

'It's a mushroom cloud,' says Emma.

'More like an oak tree,' says Dai, picking up a red to go with the blue.

'Why don't you start on your poster?' says Emma. 'Rhodri'll be along any minute,' and she holds her hand out for the coloured pencils.

'No he won't,' I say at last. 'The Headmaster's got him.' I've been waiting so long, the words come out in a rush.

'Got Rhodri? Where? Why didn't you say

before?' says Dai. He reaches in his pocket and gives Emma back the coloured pencils.

I don't get the chance to answer, because the door opens. The Headmaster comes in, steering Rhodri by the shoulder. Rhodri's feet are pumping the floor and his cheeks are pale.

'You were right,' says Emma. 'It *is* the 'Edmasta with Rhodri.'

'Good afternoon, class,' he booms at us.

We put our colouring down and chant 'Good afternoon, Mr Beynon' in the sing-song fashion teachers like. Even Rhodri joins in.

Mr Beynon squeezes Rhodri's shoulder till he squeaks. Rhodri's face is white now, and he's trying not to cry. 'I found this scallywag in the teacher's carpark, Mrs Shearer,' says Mr Beynon. 'He even informed me that you had given him permission to be there. To take deep breaths, he said. BREATHING! Scratching, more like.'

'Scratching, Mr Beynon?' says Mrs Shearer.

Mr Beynon scans the room to ensure we're getting on with our work. We all start colouring like mad. Blue mushrooms, green people.

'Scratching cars, Mrs Shearer,' says the Head-master, raising his voice and aiming it at the class. 'I discovered a scratch on the school minibus last week. Since when, I have been surveying the teacher's carpark. Today, my patience has been rewarded. My surveillance has reaped fruit in the shape of Rhodri Rhys. He thought he was safe, that no-one could see him. Little did he reckon with my binoculars. Vandals, beware.' He shakes Rhodri by the hood several times.

'Rhodri's not a vandal,' says Mrs Shearer. 'I can't believe he's been scratching cars,' she says. 'He wouldn't do anything like that. Tell the Headmaster, Rhodri. Tell him you weren't damaging any cars.'

She smiles at Rhodri. He takes a deep breath, opens his mouth, looks at the Headmaster's stern expression and says nothing. Mr Beynon glares at us to get on with our work. We colour away. The nuclear posters are beginning to look like firework night.

'Rhodri had not yet begun to perpetrate this mindless act of vandalism,' says the Headmaster. 'I nipped his intention in the bud, Mrs Shearer.' He squeezes Rhodri's shoulder again and Rhodri obliges him with a squeak. 'That is to say,' says Mr Beynon, 'I caught him before he had the chance to do anything.'

'He wasn't intending to do anything to the cars, I'm sure of it,' says Mrs Shearer. 'Tell the Headmaster, Rhodri.'

Rhodri does his drowning fish impression again.

He opens his mouth, starts to say something and stops.

'Have you nothing to say in your defence, lad?' booms Mr Beynon.

Rhodri closes his mouth.

Mr Beynon grimaces at the class before proceeding. 'This time there will be no reprisals,' he says. 'But if in the future I find Rhodri Rhys or any other pupil in the teachers' carpark, near MY CAR, there will be trouble. Henceforth, vandals like Rhodri will receive a year's continuous detention.' He looks around at our shocked expressions and adds 'Twelve entire months. The culprit will not leave the school premises for an whole year.' He glares at us, gives Rhodri a last squeeze, and goes out.

'He can't keep us in school for a year, can he?' says Ceri Evans.

'Where would we sleep?' says Emma.

'Who would feed all my animals?' says Ceri, with just a fleck of panic in his voice.

'They have to give you warning,' says Dai, 'my Nan says.'

'Mr Beynon didn't mean it,' says Andrea. 'He'd have to live in the school for an entire year to keep an eye on Rhodri, wouldn't he? No one's going to stay in a school for a whole year.'

'Of course they're not,' says Mrs Shearer.

All this time Rhodri's just standing there, silent.

Mrs Shearer looks hard at Rhodri. 'I don't understand why you didn't answer the Headmaster,' she says. 'You didn't scratch any cars, did you?'

'Course not,' says Rhodri, 'I'm not a vandal.'

'Then why didn't you explain that to the Headmaster, Rhodri?' asks Mrs Shearer, gently. 'Why didn't you tell him?'

We all wait on Rhodri's answer. We're all wondering why he hasn't protested his innocence.

'I didn't dare tell him,' says Rhodri, 'in case he put me in detention. You see, Miss, I've just been sick all over the boot of his car.'

Nicola Davies

39

Red Kite Day

Crows herald my coming.

They rise to me suddenly through the swirl of morning mist above a valley hung with woodland. Their caws are loud and raucous. They attack from all sides, harry my flight with vicious jabs of beak and wing. Glanced by a hurtle of bodies, I feel the thrum of air beneath me. I judder, tilt, adjust the fork of my tail to gain a pulse of thermal. I lift, soar spiralling, until the mob of crows are speckled far below me. My rare call, high-pitched and rapid, shrills against them.

Mine is a country of mountains. I swoop summit beyond summit, gash of valley after valley. Here rivers have their beginnings. Each rise of water is reeded, tawny as the sheen of feathers on my back.

I hold my wings motionless, slightly forward and gently arched, and watch the shadow of my outspread shape glide like cloud-race across bare uplands.

I quarter the countryside.

My hooded, amber eyes are unblinking. I seek out small movements, rabbit or vole, mouse or lizard, snake or frog. I wheel the sunlight in silence, shift direction to the twist and fan of my tail, flex one wing to bank above a jagged crop of fir trees.

I drift, beat my wings slow and deep so that the

tips of feathers almost brush beneath my breast. I am both the hawk and the swallow. No other bird, gull or crow, buzzard or harrier can match my easy buoyancy, my mastery of the sky.

Breasting a precipice, I angle my wings back, close my tail and drop across a silver glint of water that floods the valley. Wind noise is all around me. A quiver of movement—and deftly I turn to take a small bird on the wing. I feel the momentary grasp of its dying. To feed, I hold it barred in the sharp yellow of my claws.

Now I rest, invisible in tree cover, ruffle my beak through the stripes of my plumage. Midday sun is full of insect hum and the whisperings of leaves.

Floating once more into the open, I am part of each breeze and updraught, each eddy or current of air.

I am sky-dancer, cloud-skater, sun-spinner.

I wing through a turbulence over broken ground. I dip to forage across rock and peat bog and seas of purple moor-grass. Streams run shallow, rill in sudden rapids where the flick of fish attracts my eye. I dream a coolness of trout but the water here is fast, such hunting hard. I search on upstream towards a plateau of white pasture.

These high sheep walks are lonely. The one

farmstead is far below, small as a flung pebble. It teeters on the edge of a land that is different, walled and fenced and emerald. Sometime, when the winter bites harder, I'll visit that country's thrown rubbish, peck in tight backyards. Up here a sickly sheep is unprotected and disturb-ance by dog or shepherd unusual. I follow the trail of fierce-mouthed ravens who stalk the flock, leave carcasses ripped open. A stain of carrion catches my eye. I descend in eager, reducing circles, grip an exposed rib-cage. I balance, fold my wings. I bow my head and sinewy strands of meat tear between my claw and bill.

As light fades, my flight returns low down the valley, skims hawthorn hedgerows. I land in a glimmer of oak trees whose leaves are coloured copper, russet as myself in the slow closing of the sun's eye.

In early spring I'll play the wind above this meadow, tumble a mating dance. I'll weave a new nest of twigs laced with scraps of paper and plastic. I'll cosset inside it with a comfort of sheep's wool. My new nest will be secret, its dappled eggs safe from man or crow or squirrel. I think about eggs and their smooth, warm shapes. I count them in my mind, one or two or three, as I wing to roost through the coming night.

Julie Rainsbury

Winning

We all want to win. Josie used to, until she discovered that sometimes it's impossible to really win. After all, winning that school raffle was not the positive experience she had hoped it would be, what with her best friend, Tess, not speaking to her for a week, and her arch-enemy, Dawn Davies, having a field day at her expense.

Tess, Tess. What a great girl. Josie had met her on her first day at school and been bowled over by her directness. 'Hello,' she had said, 'my name's Tess. Will you be my friend?' Impressed to the point of dumbness by such confidence from a fellow four-year old, and on such a day, Josie had eventually managed to stammer out a feeble 'Yes'. Looking back, Josie was sure she could remember feeling uneasy even then. The big adventure of her first day was being taken out of her hands. Suddenly the large classroom she was so keen to explore shrank to the size of a chairspace between her and Tess, and yet she was pleased too—pleased to have been sought out by her and pleased to have something, already, to tell her mother at hometime.

More than four years after this first meeting, Josie entered the raffle. With the money given to them by their mothers turning sweaty in their hands, she and Tess queued to buy their threepenny tickets, the prize then unknown. The best donation to the school Bring and Buy Sale was to be held back to be the prize. The anticipation of winning was heightened by conjecture over what the grand prize was to be. Eight year old minds ran riot with exotic possibilities.

When Josie saw Tess on that first day she had a feeling of having seen her in a book somewhere. She looked so perfect with her hair in long plaits which she wore hooked-up and tied with bows at the sides of her head, like door knockers. She had shop clothes, not home-made like Josie's, and looked complete and self-contained. She smelled of milk and had a pocket in her knickers. Josie could not have been more impressed.

A couple of days later, Miss Norris came into the classroom to talk to Josie's class teacher, who immediately switched from English to that secret language of teachers, the one they always used so that the pupils would not know what was being said. Miss Norris's message, once translated, was that Josie should go at once to see Mrs Evans in Standard I.

In the cosmopolitan streets of Josie's Cardiff, she heard many dialects and tongues, but Welsh was not among them. She was much more likely to hear Italian, Greek or Spanish spoken by her neighbours, for those who taught her at school lived far away from the streets she knew. So it took Josie some years to discover that Welsh was not a secret language taught only to trainee teachers, but a language which lived outside schools and held the key to the strange-sounding songs which she learned parrot-fashion and sang on St. David's Day.

Josie went, as instructed, to the Standard I cabin classrooms, which stood in the playground and were known as The Huts, where she was told that she had won the raffle. It was wonderful news! She did not hear much of the rest of what Mrs Evans said to her. 'I've won, I've won,' was all that filled her mind and her head seemed to fizz with the knowledge. Then Mrs Evans gave her the prize. It was a large rubber doll in a turquoise coloured dress, with tight curly blonde hair and a huge inkstain on her cheek. She was not really disappointed, not at first, even though she did not play with dolls very much and despite the obvious used look it had. The winning was enough, it was, it was, but even as she carried the doll back across the playground, Josie started to feel awkward with it.

Her teacher was pleased at her news and Josie enjoyed the minor fuss it afforded her, but felt more and more unhappy as she looked at the bland rubbery face and enormous blue smudge. She began to feel she was being made a fool of.

She returned to her desk, opened her mouth to

speak but left her lower lip hanging as Tess pointedly turned her face to the wall, her door knockers swinging gently, but firmly, to let Josie know the position. She sat down, very red in the face, and tried to stuff the hideous doll under the desk and out of the way. She succeeded in that, but not in getting Tess to talk to her. She kept up a barrage of silence which shelled Josie mercilessly for the rest of the day. You had to admire such resolve.

Tess was always determined—and perverse. Then, under-fives were dosed daily with cod liver oil, 'to make them strong'. Most children breathed a sigh of relief on their fifth birthday, but not Tess. She still stood in the queue awaiting her spoonful and was even known to return to the end of the line for a second dose. Josie did not know which amazed her more, how Tess could swallow the stuff, or have the nerve to cheat the system.

The dinner bell rang and Josie rushed to leave school with the awful doll. She wanted no-one to see her with it and she felt she had to get it as far away as possible from Tess. Maybe distance from the prize would make her forget her anger with Josie. She rounded the corner of The Huts, and found her way squarely blocked by Dawn Davies —who, if not exactly the school bully, was at least Josie's bully. There was no way of knowing what

46

singled out Josie for her hatred, but it was keen and real and they both acknowledged it without question.

'Wer d'you think yaw gowin to wi tha doll?' Dawn squawked at her. Josie saw that Dawn had a very nervous-looking Helen Morris in tow.

'I'm takin' ir 'ome. I wun ir in thu rafful,' she replied, hating the stupid, ink-stained thing more than ever.

'S'Elen's doll,' retorted Dawn. 'Er mam giv i tu thu sa-ul an she din' no nuthink abowri', didjew, 'El?'

'Umm, no,' came the hesitant reply.

Swallowing both fear and outrage at this latest onslaught from Dawn, Josie responded with a much too smug:

'Well, she must 'ave, else 'ow did i' ge' tu skoo-ul?'

Dawn jabbed at Josie's shoulder with her finger as she replied:

'Yeh, bu' she din' no i' wuz gowin'-u be the prize, di' she?'

'I' down' marrer. She brought irrin so is norr'ers no maw.'

It was funny how this doll that Josie now loathed for cheating her of a real prize and, worse, for coming between her and Tess, was suddenly important. If she had been unable to offer it through generosity to Tess, then it was impossible to give it, through fear, to Dawn. Absolute fear of Dawn Davies ruled Josie's life, and absolute fear must make it unthinkable to give in to her. Quaking in her shoes, cheeks burning, Josie tried to move off, now clutching the doll as if it were her most prized possession. Helen Morris looked instantly relieved and went to walk away too, but Dawn slid an insistent, scheming arm around her and held her fast. They stood facing each other, Dawn clasping Helen, and Josie clutching the doll.

'If yew don' give i' back, I'm gowin' a tell on yew.'

'There's nuthin tu tell. Mr Evans give i' tu me. I's thu prize.'

'I' down marrer. I's 'Elen's, and she goroo 'av i' back, so.'

Josie stood her ground. That doll suddenly meant *everything* to her. She'd been swindled out of a decent prize, ostracised by Tess and now tormented by the girl who could turn any day into a nightmare. How *could* she give it up? It would make nonsense of all that she had gone through and, behind this thought, an insistent, nagging belief was forming in Josie's mind—it was her *right* to keep it! Nothing was going to take from her what fate and a threepenny raffle ticket had brought her. Tess was being unfair, Dawn Davies

48

was being unfair, being awarded a rotten stupid doll with a stupid dirty face was unfair, but taking from her what she had fairly won was no justice at all! Suddenly indignant and angry, Josie pushed with all her strength against Dawn Davies and, catching her by surprise, managed to run off as Dawn reeled backwards from the shove and collapsed in a heap with Helen on top of her.

Josie went straight home alone. Tess had gone with the others. And the doll stayed at home when Josie came back after dinner.

For the whole of the rest of the week, Tess sulked about that doll. For the first time in her life, Josie had stood up to that nasty Dawn Davies and Tess hadn't even shown whose side she was on! Just to think of it make Josie burn with that indignation that makes eyes prick and huge pebbles gather in the throat.

It was only after the weekend break that things began to ease. Josie found her resentment fading and she began to lose her appetite for fanning its flames. Tess had, in any case, lost interest in the doll and in the battle between them. In time they slid back into their old, easy way with one another, but they never spoke of the doll again.

Dawn Davies's antagonism towards Josie became legendary in time. At high school, Tess would recount to friends how Dawn used to say to her 'An' I 'ates that

Josie Dobbs. I 'ates 'er, me.' By that time, Josie was compelled to laugh along with the others, but the story always made her uneasy, as much for the intimacy it implied between Tess and Dawn as for the memories of past persecution it stirred up.

Several weeks after the raffle, with the whole incident almost completely faded in Josie's mind, she and Tess were dawdling their way home from school. They had stopped at Old Ma's dim and dingy drinks shop and queued for ten minutes or so at the counter. They called it 'the bar' and would slap their ha'pennies or tuppences down on it like cowboys in a saloon as they ordered their drinks of sarsaparilla or lemonade. They were served in Shippam's paste pots of varying size, according to the order. Old Ma, slovenly and repulsive, and therefore fascinating, would swill them in a bowl of soapy water between customers. The girls downed their drinks like seasoned gunslingers, then wiped their lips on the backs of their hands.

Sauntering out into the glare of the street, their pace was set for the rest of the trip home. Casually turning the corner by the block of flats, they came face to face with Dawn Davies. As they stopped to receive her abuse, Josie noticed an older girl to the side. It was Dilys Watts from the secondary school. She was standing on the small boundary wall which circled the flats and, as she spotted her, Josie saw and felt, simultaneously it seemed, the long metal chain handle of Dilys's shoulder bag whipping across the backs of her knees. There was no longer any doubt. Josie had won nothing on the day they drew that raffle.

When she was a sixth former, Josie took a holiday job in Mackross, a department store now torn down, in the centre of Cardiff. Her childhood seemed far behind her (she was even studying that secret teachers' language at A-Level). On her last day in the job, Josie saw a young woman choosing curtains with her mother. Josie went over to serve them and bent down to smile at the toddler in a buggy which the young woman was pushing. She looked up at the mother and felt the shock of old, and by now unfamiliar, tremors as she realised that it was Dawn Davies.

Dawn was as nice as pie, and so, of course, was Josie.

And Tess? She and Josie are still friends. She lives in Manchester with her three daughters, but has no pocket in her knickers and has not touched cod liver oil in years. Not long ago, Josie mentioned the raffle incident to her. Tess could not remember it.

Debbie Groves

Dicko, Me and the Mystery Circle

It was Dicko who came up with The Idea that day, the longest and hottest day of a long, long summer. We were sitting on a bench in the Square next to Dai Jinks who was reading a paper. His lips were moving anyway. Dicko was reading it too.

' "Corn Circles Mystery Moves to East Anglia," ' he read out. 'Funny we don't get corn circles around here.'

'Nobody grows corns,' I said.

'Why do the circles have to be in corn?' demanded Dicko. 'They could be made up there on the side of the mountain, in the ferns. Let's do it,' he said. Just like that.

'Why?' I asked.

Dicko and me have been buddies since we were in Infants' School and I've learned one lesson in the eight years since then. It doesn't do to agree too soon to any of Dicko's ideas.

'Because it's boring sitting here,' he said. 'Let's see if we can stir things up a bit and make a headline story ourselves.'

'Fair enough,' I said.

The mountain, Cilfach yr Encil, is also called

the Hang Gliders' Hill because of the dare-devil strangers who come to take running jumps off the top of it. They look pretty, mind, when they float off up on their red and blue wings, like gigantic coloured moths. The Welsh Air Force we call them.

'How can we do it?' asked Dicko. He'd had The Idea, but I had to work it out. T'was ever thus, as Mr Davies History says.

'How do we make a circle in geometry?' I asked.

'With compasses and pencil,' said Dicko, quick as a flash. 'But that would be too small, stupid, to use up the mountain.'

'Don't be daft, mun, it's the principle of the thing,' I said. 'How does Uncle Harry make circles in his garden for his night-scented stock?'

'He puts one stick in the middle with a string tied to it and another stick on the other end of the string and he draws a . . .'

'Circle,' I finished for him. 'We'll do the same thing only we'll have to have a big stick in the middle and a longer piece of string.'

We borrowed the string from Uncle Harry's allotment shed. He caught us borrowing.

'What do you want that for?' he asked.

'To tie up a parcel for Mam,' I said.

'How much do you want?' he said bringing out

his Stanley knife. He thinks the world of our Mam.

'Fifteen feet,' I said.

'Blooming big parcel,' he grumbled. 'What're you boys up to?' But he cut off a good long length and gave it to us without any more questions.

'We'll have to wait till it's dark to go up the mountain.' I said. I told you it was summer. It didn't get dark till about ten o'clock.

'I'll be over at Dicko's until late, Mam,' I said. Dicko told his Ma he'd be over with me.

Where do you hide fifteen feet of hairy string when you're only wearing jeans and a tee shirt? I wrapped it around my middle and hoped no-one would notice the bulge. It was a bit rough on my skin, especially where I'd caught the sun. I met Dicko at the allotment shed and there we waited, jawing as usual, until it was darkish.

When we couldn't see our faces properly any more we went up through the *gwli* behind Chapel Street and joined the path up the mountain. Just below Eagle Rock we struck diagonally across the hillside moving cautiously through the ferns. They came up to our shoulders almost.

'We should have brought machetes to hack through this lot,' whispered Dicko.

'No, we mustn't show we've been here. That's the mystery of it,' I whispered back.

'Fat chance we'd have of getting hold of machetes anyway,' he breathed.

'This is far enough,' I said later, and stopped to unwrap the string . Could I find the end of it? No. Dicko got impatient.

'Here let me have a go,' he said and fumbled around my middle. It tickled and I doubled up with my elbows close to my sides and cracked laughing. I couldn't help it.

'Shut up,' hissed Dicko. 'I've got it now. Hey, we've forgotten the stick for the centre of the circle.'

'No sweat,' I said, getting my breath back. 'I'll stand in the middle and turn round as you unwind away from me. When it comes to the end I'll tug three times and you start off in a clockwise direction and walk over the ferns, keeping the string tight so you'll know you're going in a proper ring.'

'OK,' said Dicko and swished off through the ferns. I kept on turning and turning on the spot until the string came off. I grabbed the end and tugged to signal Dicko to start walking around in a circle. There was a distant trampling sound which I took to be Dicko trampling the ferns flat.

There was a scream and someone gave a loud

shout. A startled Dicko came crashing back, dragging the string behind him. We both took off, sharpish.

When we were back in the *gwli* I asked 'What happened?'

'I'd only gone about thirty steps when I trod on a couple,' he said.

'A couple of what?' I asked.

'A courting couple, birdbrain,' he said.

'We'll try again tomorrow night,' I said.

'No way Ho Zay,' said Dicko.

'Stands to reason they won't be there tomorrow,' I said. 'Being trodden on by you is enough to kill anyone's urge for a love life. Anyway to be on the safe side we'll go in disguise.'

'What disguise?'

'I'll think of something,' I said.

'Clare's laddered her tights and chucked 'em in the bin,' I told Dicko the following day. 'So what?' said Dicko. He doesn't like my sister much.

'I've sneaked 'em. I'll cut 'em in half and we can wear a leg each. If anyone sees us it'll make us look weird, like something from Outer Space,' I said.

'You look weird already,' said Dicko. That was unkind. He knows I'm a bit shy about my zits. 'And I'm not wearing any sister's tights. In any case what about the rest of our bodies? We can't just disguise our faces. People'll know us by our tee shirts.'

'Long macks and wellies,' I said.

The next night we said we'd be at Malc's, but we didn't tell Malc. He can't keep his mouth shut.

We arranged to meet near the Eagle Rock. I was early. My Dad's mack hung well below the tops of his wellies which were loose on my feet. My nose, flattened under the champagne beige of Clare's wrecked tights, was beginning to itch. Through the mist of nylon I could just see a strange figure moving towards me.

It was horrible. A gleaming white thing it was, and headless.

It was Dicko wearing his Ma's lollipop lady coat and with his head submerged in a black balaclava.

'Got the string?' he asked, his voice muffled in wool.

'Yeah.' I answered through stiff lips.

We'd taken a bearing of where we'd been the night before from a solitary may tree on the skyline and an ash tree near the abandoned Lido. The Lido had been the only swimming pool in the place in the 1930s my dad had told me. It used to be filled with icy water from the mountain stream. Five minutes in that was enough to give cramp to anyone's style, my Dad said.

We got back to where we'd been before, or

near enough, and I took the piece of string from the pocket of my mack. Dicko set off holding the looped end tight around his right wrist. We both held the string high so as not to disturb the ferns within the circle.

I stood still, resisting the uneven pulls as he made his way around like an erratic hour hand. It took an age. I could hear the fern stems snapping. When he came full circle he made his way back to me.

'It's no good,' he said. 'The ferns spring back and cover the path I've made.'

'No sweat,' I said. 'I'll think of something.'

We went down the mountain, packed our disguises into plastic bags, put them in the shed, and said 'See you,' quietly, when we got to the Square.

The next night we had to write off because I had to help Dad water the garden and he wouldn't do it until the sun went down over the mountain, too late for us to fix up anything. But it gave me time to ponder the problem, as my Dad says sometimes. Not often, mind.

When we met at the top of the *gwli*, Dicko was in his lollipop lady's coat again. I had my mack and wellies and carried a broom handle.

'So?' he said, looking at it.

'We stick the broom handle in the middle with

the string tied to it and walk around in a circle side by side. It'll widen the mystery track,' I explained.

'Cool,' he said.

After shifting the stone we'd left to mark the middle of the ring, we jammed the broom handle into the turf and with Dicko holding the string up high, we went backwards away from the centre.

'Don't pull too hard or we'll have the broom handle out,' I warned.

'You do it then,' he said, so I did.

We set off, Dicko and me, side by side. He found the first sketchy path he'd made and, with a bit of extra wellie, we tamped it down a bit more, widened it, and made it more obvious. Then we rolled up the string, and made for home.

Next morning the blackbird shattered the silence first as usual and I went to the bedroom to see if I could see our Mystery Circle. It was there all right, a smaller circle than I'd thought it would be considering the effort it cost us, but it was clear enough if you were looking in the right direction. I told Dicko. He couldn't see it from his side of the village. He came over to my place and looked over, casual like, across the valley. 'Anyone noticed it yet?'

'No, not yet,' I said.

No-one noticed it all day.

We'd have to do some prodding. Mrs Jones, Tŷ Gwyn was our best bet. Mrs Jones believed in Flying Saucers because she'd seen one and told the local paper about it. A reporter had come down to interview her and indeed there was her picture in the paper the next week, taken with her standing in front of her Dorothy Perkins roses and pointing to the sky.

'It was shining and round and moved backwards and forwards, not a bit like an aircraft,' she had told the reporter.

The reporter had also got a comment from a weather man who said it was probably a Met Office balloon. But Mrs Jones wouldn't hear of it being a balloon.

'He didn't see it. I did,' she said to the neighbours when the story came out. 'It was an Unidentified Flying Object if ever I saw one.'

It was handy that Mrs Jones was there already on the doorstep looking for gossip.

'Hullo Mrs Jones,' I said. 'Seen any UFOs lately?' I was serious, not taking the mick. She hadn't. 'Heard about the corn circles?' I asked. She had. 'How do you reckon they're made?' I asked.

'Flying Saucers of course,' she said. 'They come straight down from up there, with a sort of skirt, like a hovercraft, only it's stiff, so when it lands it leaves a perfect circle.'

'Wouldn't they leave burn marks with their retro rockets, Mrs J?' asked Dicko.

'Superconductivity,' said Mrs Jones. And I knew she'd been listening to an Open University talk on Radio 4 FM, my Dad's favourite wavelength. It had been on in our house too.

'Me and Dicko noticed something funny on the mountain over by Eagle Rock,' I said.

'Never!' said Mrs Jones, intrigued.

'See if you can see anything,' I tempted.

She came over the road and looked up across the valley. 'I can see a sheep track,' she said pointing out a diagonal line that went up to the mountain top.

'Over to the right, Mrs J,' prompted Dicko making a big play of holding his hand over his eyes to shield them from the sun.

'I see it,' she cried. 'In among the ferns. It's a circle. It's a Mystery Circle, like they've been getting up England way.'

'You'd better phone the paper,' suggested Dicko.

'Indeed I will,' said Mrs Jones and off she went back into her house.

We didn't hang around there. We went to the Square. In a while a newspaper van drove through.

We went after it, but not too close, because we didn't want to be asked questions. Looking around the corner we saw two people get out, a girl with a notebook and a bored looking man with a camera bag. Mrs Jones came to the door. She'd taken her pinny off and combed her hair.

She took the two visitors across the road and pointed. The man took her picture. Then he aimed a shot along her pointing arm to where the circle was.

'He's trying for an off-beat angle,' said Dicko knowledgeably.

People stopped to find out what was going on and Mrs Jones was pleased to tell them. They really hadn't believed in her UFO story but now they couldn't disbelieve their own eyes for the Mystery Circle was there for all to see.

Dicko and I went back to the Square.

'Where've you been lately?' asked Malc.

'Mind your own . . .' I said.

The paper came out two days later. Mrs Jones was there on the front page this time and there, too, was the smudgy shape of our Mystery Circle.

'Magic Circle Mystery' read the headline. 'A mysterious circle has magically appeared overnight among the ferns growing on Mynydd Cilfach yr Encil,' it reported. It went on to quote Mrs Jones (she forgot to say it was brought to her attention by two village boys—we were relieved at that!) Mr Jenkins, the farmer whose land it was on (' . . . don't want any trespassers, from Outer Space or anywhere else, worrying my sheep . . .') and a police spokesman who said it appeared to be the work of light hearted hoaxers. Light hearted? It was the most serious work we'd done so far, Dicko and me.

'What about creating a pentagram? We might make the nationals with that,' said Dicko.

'Let me ponder the problem,' I said.

I'm still working on it.

Anne Ahmad

Catching the Wave

I was never really popular, especially with children my own age. My friends were known for their abilities—football, tennis, rugby, piano competitions. They all seemed to have goals, achievements they could talk about or accept praise for. I liked going off on my own. I could draw and catch fish. But to others these pastimes were 'boring'. Whenever I look back at this stage in my life a certain sentence springs to mind:

'He's nothing like his brother, is he?'

Peter, my cool, popular brother, had been my idol for as long as I could remember. Long hair, deafening rock music, dangerous hobbies and a lot of friends. He was everything I wanted to be, but I never thought it possible to match his success or way of life. The summer I was twelve, he seemed to me a symbol of freedom, a sort of town 'beach bum', surfing all day and going to wild beach parties by night, but somehow still managing to get A grades at college during the week. He was still my parents' blue-eyed boy, and he had plenty of smiles for them, but he'd become off-hand with me. His lack of interest in me made me angry. I suppose I was jealous and it made me spiteful and offensive towards him when we had to do things 'as a family' as my mother put it.

At last I saw that I would have to give surfing a shot.

It wasn't easy, though I was a strong swimmer. 'I can't do this,' I must have told myself hundreds of times as I hauled my aching body out of the breakers, eyes and mouth full of salt, and started all over again. Balancing on a narrow, boisterous surfboard was the hardest thing I had ever attempted. The defeats hurt mentally as well as physically but I wasn't a failure and I wouldn't give up. Anger and loneliness turned to aggression, I fought hard and my jealousy was like an engine inside me. Determination grew.

Four weeks into that summer of '89 I finally got the hang of it. Skimming along the surface of a big wave was incredible. The only thing I'd ever known like it was sliding down the bannisters at my grandparents' home, a forbidden challenge. It was frightening too, living on the edge. One mistake could be fatal but the surge of adrenalin controlled my body. For the first time, I felt dominant. And vulnerable. Riding wild on the back of a beast that would throw me and swallow me whole, learning to read the buck and thrum of the board through my feet—where do I go? Which way do I turn? Sometimes my body guessed right; more often, I was tossed aside like a plastic bag in the wind, rolled and pummelled and spat out. But every wave I caught was teaching me, building my confidence until I felt ready for the test. A new world had opened in front of me and I couldn't wait to be appreciated.

'The Marine' was where my brother and his mates surfed. The waves were bigger, more dangerous. This was the beach where locals and outsiders gathered, to surf, sunbathe or just watch.

All eyes were turned to the sea, that glittering arena where reputations were made or lost, where hopes soared with the swooping figures balanced precariously on their boards, or plummeted and disappeared into the swell. Here, every mistake would be noted, each slip or triumph re-lived over and again. It was my big chance. My mouth was dry as I imagined carrying my board down the beach, paddling out with the waves trying to push me back to shore, waiting there for a good swell. With my back to all those eyes.

Summer was going quickly. If I was going to find the guts to do it, it had to be soon. Then, one hot night, I dreamed about going fishing. I was at my secret, secluded pool again, and it was about to change something inside me, as it had four years before, helping me along the road to a happier childhood.

Dad had been a very keen fisherman, and he'd passed on his enthusiasm to me when I was still quite young. But though I listened, and copied him and did all the right things, I'd never caught anything, and somehow I got it into my head that he looked on me as a failure. One afternoon, I set off on my own to the river, determined to try all I could to prove myself.

A thick blanket of branches and leaves made a cave from the sunlight except for the odd burst that escaped the grasp of the overhanging trees to flicker on the deep, dark water. Multicoloured leaves glided past in the tranquil flow of the river.

I sat tensely on the muddy bank dangling the worm into the unreadable depths, waiting. Crouched intent as a predator, I waited silently, trying not to think of all the times I had disappointed my father by failing to capture one of the elusive streamlined creatures that I knew were cruising in the shadows. I imagined their wariness as they nuzzled through the weed, avoiding the patches of dancing light, perhaps looking up through the magnifying water at my large, still shape and trying to work out if it meant danger. I remembered walking into the kitchen all those other Sunday afternoons to the smell of freshly caught trout.

Suddenly my rod jerked, then started vibrating rapidly in my sweaty palms. I reeled in the line slowly and fought as hard as an eight-year-old could. I was frightened and angry. I needed this fish desperately, and hung on as he darted and thrashed. I was thinking of Dad. His voice echoed in my head, encouraging me not to let go, as he had so many times, before turning away with a sigh or silent shrug. I wasn't struggling with the fish but with the recognition between me and my father.

I scurried along the bank and picked up my net. A net in one hand, and then a trout, slippery silver, in the other. It was in the landing net and bigger than I had first imagined it to be. A magnificent fish. I felt like crying. I wasn't a failure.

The house was quiet and still. Mum and Dad were out walking in the park and Pete was still on the beach. I found the silver tray and placed my catch on it ceremoniously as my father used to.

This time it was Dad's turn to smell the freshly-caught trout when he walked into the kitchen. I can't recall his exact words, but I had never been so happy in all my life. I felt that from this day on, he believed in me and what I could accomplish. I not only caught a fish that day but also the attention I had been missing from my father.

The morning after the fishing dream, I knew I was ready.

I remember exactly how it felt, catching my

first wave on that beach crowded with surfers. In the distance, I saw the first small shiver and lift of the sunlit water, like a big mouth opening and closing. Paddling out, I could feel the sea's energy pulling at me, stronger than usual, the backwash dragging me down as the breakers surged shorewards. Surfacing, at first I saw nothing, blinded by salt, then it was there, the big one, the whole horizon bulging, and I was being lifted like a cork. I flipped round, pointed myself to the land, and then it was under me, the long curving uneven back of the monster I was flying.

I knew their eyes were following me as I rode it, hearing its thunder and feeling its power thrilling in my firmly-planted feet. I felt special and unique, like a god who ruled the ocean and knew all there was to know about surfing. The sun blazed against my freckled skin, trying to dazzle me with its rainbows in the spray as the wave splashed me with the last of its strength. I expect it was this and the eyes of all the onlookers that caused the flush that scorched my face. Plus the warm, anxious look from my brother.

I had arrived.

Sion Williams

The Blue Man

Every Friday I'd wheel my bike up the path and lean it against the wooden steps that led to the door. By that time the wetter and colder I was, the happier. My paper-sack was empty, and a saucepan of *cawl* was steaming for me on the ancient Aga. I can still see it. Vivid bits of leek, carrot and turnip bobbing in the bowl, and home-made rolls, all shapes, freckled like the old ladies' hands. One of them would stoop to lift the rolls from the oven with a tea towel, leaning her other hand against her knee to help her straighten up as she turned, smiling, wiping the flour on her pinny. Her sisters would take my coat, give me a hug, sit me down at the table. My mother didn't approve. Weird, she called them. I never got bowls of lamb *cawl* or hugs at home.

It was the last call on my round, last house on the beach road before it fizzled out in a track between sand dunes. Villagers called it the Last House, but at school it was known as Finches' Cottage, a rambling wooden bungalow with a veranda that ran all around it. It boomed like a dull drum, thudded, rattled and breathed. Every footstep echoed on the boards of the long central corridor, filling the rooms with vibrations. The house crackled in frost and creaked in the sun. In winter the wind off the dunes shook and thumped it, sand-blasting the paint from the walls. Outside you could hear the wind whistling in the marram grass, stinging the windows, and a deeper sound like waves breaking in the elms at the edge of the convent lawn. I'd forgotten the elms. Dutch Elm disease must have got them by now. Ghost trees. Does the bell hang in a dead tree? And the nun who used to pull the bell rope morning and evening? Where has she gone? It gives me the creeps to think about things like that.

The autumn after my twelfth birthday, when my mother moved to live in town after the split, I became a boarder. It was a brand-new life. There were only twenty boarders, and to my delight three of us were lodged at Finches' Cottage. It wasn't like being a proper boarder. I had a room of my own, and I was allowed to keep my paper round. My sister went with my mother. The only snag with sleeping at Finches was the walk back from school in the pitch dark after homework. Through the orchard, past the log-shed where the headless man lurked, through the gap in the wall, down steps cut in the rock on which the convent was built, and a scurry down the paved path to the bungalow door. We never thought of torches.

Two Misses Finch and Mrs Price. Three sisters.

They had been teachers and had travelled the world. One used to be a missionary till she had her doubts about God. I didn't let the nuns know this, as I wasn't sure about God myself and I didn't want a sermon. On the board floors of their wide wooden house, painted green and cream like a shelter in the park, were rugs in old deep reds and inky blues. There were ivory elephants, which I didn't tell my friends about, carved African heads, and a case of wonderful butterflies. The butterflies on the dunes were like little flags in the wind and you couldn't see them properly. The ones in the case were brilliant as stained glass, so real they might be quivering.

I stopped telling my mother about the Finches. She despised their 'untidiness', what she called 'all those things'. But I was going to have a house like theirs. It was the most beautiful house in the world. I looked at the treasures on Sunday nights by the fire as I ate the treats they saved for me when the younger girls had gone to bed. They had a book of Welsh poetry bound in green leather. It was hand-printed on hand-made paper with rough edges, and on every sheet you could see a pale pattern like a little sickle when you held it against the light. I loved paper. I went in for fancy writing paper, mauve, scented, bevel edged, for long letters to pen-friends full of not quite true descriptions of my life. The initials to the poems in the book were printed in dark red, but best of all were the pictures: engravings of waterfalls, woods, whirlpools and lovers. They made me ache. I had a book that made me feel like that when I was little, but my mother threw it out. I liked the poem book's mysterious language, like a secret code. I knew some of the words, remembered from long-lost Taid who died when I was three. My mother kept her meanest voice for Welsh, probably because of her and Dad not getting on. She had a specially snobbish way of saying 'Welsh!' So one day I intended to learn it.

Elder Miss Finch had collected the books, younger Miss Finch the rugs and butterflies. The Finches were thin and blue-eyed and wore their grey hair in plaits. The elder divided her hair in a single parting from forehead to nape and her plaits began behind her ears, their ends united in a coronet on top of her head. The younger made her plaits into a bun like a pile of rope. They all had red cheeks and wore dark blue fisherman's jumpers for walking through the dunes to the sea. Mrs Price was the youngest, and had white curls. She was plumper than the Finches, untidier, prettier, and jollier. They were all untidy according to my mother, their hair flying like silver grasses, especially when they came up from the beach in the evenings with the sun behind them, flat sandals scuffing the sand, after an afternoon at the summerhouse.

The summerhouse! The bungalow was the last real house on the road, but half a mile on at the very edge of the sea stood a wobbly row of salt-and-sand-blasted huts, leased to fishermen and summer visitors. The Finches had one. They gave me a key and said I could use it to 'study'. I went there once to do my homework. I drank a flask of tea, sat in a whiskery old wicker chair, and waited for something marvellous to happen. I felt scared. Neglected buildings are sad. When they're a bit scruffy they're friendly, then the roof or the windows go and the ghosts move in. I don't want gardens to get all brambly, houses to have broken windows, or people to die. I didn't want Taid to die, or Dad to leave, or my favourite book to be given away. I was scared of the salt-stained glass, the faded cloth at the window, the blistered paint, bladderwrack, rope, driftwood, bird-skulls and oily feathers which cluttered the creepy spaces underneath its legs. It was good when the sun shone, but when shadows came I was glad to scuff home through the soft sand for school tea, jam and sandwiches and choir practice.

At Finches Cottage that Sunday night my *cawl* and rolls were ready. The younger girls had gone to bed. I told the sisters I'd done three drawings and my English essay. That pleased them. They opened the cabinet and Mrs Price took out her flints and ammonites and shards of pottery. I've saved this bit up. Mr Price was an archaeologist. They'd lived in Bolivia and he died there. In Bolivia Mrs Price had money, but their government wouldn't let her bring it home. Which would I have chosen? Bolivia, and all the money and treasures you could imagine? Or the Last House? She enjoyed talking about the Bolivian money she would never have. I planned to rescue it for her.

She took out the treasures one by one. I held them, read the little labels and replaced them with exaggerated care. I was allowed to hold anything. Only one object seemed to me too wonderful to touch. This I have saved up till last of all to touch, and last to tell. That special evening Mrs Price lifted the object from its place, held it out to me, and laid it in my hands. A figure five inches tall made of a deep blue mineral. How heavy he was! How cold! She showed me how to turn him slowly away, and how he seemed to smile as the light moved from his gaze to his profile. Again and again I turned him, and he smiled, and slowly back to see his smile diminish. Once someone has smiled at you, you can't forget it. The face has chosen you. Under his tiny plinth was a label marked, in the archaeologist's hand-writing, 'Circa 1100, BC, Egyptian'. He was bald, standing with one foot before the other, his arms folded, 'Lapis Lazuli blue', said Mrs Price. 'A grave god'. Lapis Lazuli! What was he like, her young, dead archaeologist? Black curly hair, I decided, and lapis lazuli eyes. That was when I gave up the idea of being a vet, or a famous novelist. I would be an archaeologist.

My birthday came. I was let off maths homework, the cook made me a cake, and they sang Happy Birthday at tea. I had notepaper with a country scene, a five-year diary, a book about horses, *David Copperfield* by Charles Dickens, and scented soap. And fourteen cards. My mother sent me money. That night there was a little party at Finches. There was a big glass bowl of trifle decorated with tiny silver balls, and a huge chocolate cake on a lacy paper doily on a silver plate. When all the clocks struck eleven, out of tune with each other as usual, I thought it was over and we'd all be sent to bed. The other two girls went to their room, and I was kept back. They wanted a word with me. Footsteps thumped up and down the corridor between the bedroom and the bathroom. Miss Finch with the coiled rope put on Beethoven's 'Moonlight Sonata'. They'd taught me to enjoy things like that. As I told my friends, you've just got to give it a try. Miss Finch with the coronet took out the book of Welsh poems. Mrs Price poured me a very small sherry in a lovely glass that twinkled like diamonds. 'You're a teenager now!' She beamed at me. They'd never given me sherry before. I wouldn't mention this in school. 'We want you to have a present,' she said. I felt hot and excited. I was the favourite. Any minute now a black haired hero with lapis lazuli eyes would arrive. He was already on the road, riding a black horse, or perhaps driving a red sports car.

Mrs Price took the key to the Bolivian archaeologist's case. She opened it. 'I am old,' she said, 'and I know you like these things. Choose something.' I held little pieces of pottery, thinking I would love any of them but for the alluring blue gaze of the little Egyptian grave god. I wished they'd put him away so I could think properly. 'I don't like to say,' I said. 'I don't want to choose something you love too much.' 'Choose!' said Mrs Price. 'It's something we love we want you to have. We can't take them with us when we go.' I felt sick. When they go. Like everyone else they would go. I concentrated hard again. He was already chosen but I dared not say. Last of all I weighed him in my hand until his coldness was lost and he was blood-warm. I looked at their faces. They were twinkling. One Miss Finch knitted. The other embroidered. Mrs Price looked at me. 'I love him,' I said at last.

'And we love you, my dear,' said Mrs Price, reaching beside her chair. She picked up a wooden box, an inch longer than the blue man, lined with cotton wool that fitted him so exactly that she must have known all the time that I'd choose him.

'To remember us,' she beamed.

I couldn't speak. I wouldn't tell anyone about the blue man, or the tears.

That was years ago. I'm in my first year at University now, doing English, Welsh and Archaeology, and I'm off to the museum to have him valued. At least, I think I am. A couple of times I've been on the brink of asking an expert in antiquities to value him. Then he'd ask, 'Have you something to show me?' 'No', I'd say. 'Just looking.'

I have a terrible confession to make. I've lost the Finches, sort of mislaid them. I left school to do A levels in the college. I wrote to them once. I'd given up scented stationery and had found somewhere you could buy hand made paper. The shop was shut. I would write again when the shop was open. After A levels I went to India, trekking with a friend. I wrote from Delhi. I came back to find my letter returned with 'not known at this address' on it. I was afraid to go back to look for them.

In my head is a derelict house full of the sea wind, and round it the world is falling to ruin. I can hardly breathe. I turn away from the museum desk to check, deep in my bag, for the wooden box. I can't wait to get home, take him out of the box, hold him till he's blood-warm, and be forgiven.

Gillian Clarke

A Welsh Country Childhood

Gathering wild strawberries in a cooling down summer lane, past Gelli bridge and the stream gossiping over stones. Frothing honeysuckle clinging to hedges, smelling of heaven in the gathering dusk. Rooks laughing in trees, charcoal black against the sinking orange sun. No noise except cows ripping grass and breathing heavily and a thrush singing lullabies to the day.

Back to Gelli Farm with Gwen, up the steps to her tidy house, with the smell of home grown apples in boxes coming from her front room. Pale lilac dyed nets, very posh. Gwen, her eyes dark as whinberries, pulls on her white cardigan over a mauve gingham dress. Oh, envy! Into the back kitchen where her mother is drinking tea and smoking, listening to the wireless. Gwen shows me her new shoes—they have real heels, and no six month guarantee. My shoes are indestructible. She doesn't have to wear a woolly vest either with tell tale sleeves and rubber buttons that make lumps in your dress.

I have to go now, it's nearly dark. Gwen comes out to the road to wave me goodbye, and as I walk away, I turn round and wave back. She is standing under the snowball tree and her white cardigan is showing off in the dark.

Up the road past the telephone poles, wires full of humming Martians and my heart is beating loud enough to hear. Fast as I can go to the top of the hill, walking backwards all the way to make sure that no one is behind me. The fields are lying down asleep under a pale turquoise sky, and the sun has left an orange tinge, just to show there's no ill feeling. Past the milk churns, down the track to Gaerwen Farm past where the harebells grow caps for fairies, past the cowed dogs, Bell, Gay and Fly crouching on their bellies, tails wagging.

Past the farm house with one dim lamp-lit window, glowing like an eye. Over the brook and down into the dark woods, where bears and wolves live. Behind the trees they are, I can hear them breathing. Run, run like the wind, towards my house, Tilly lamp lit. Run through the moonlight-dappled woods before the *Ladi Wen* gets me. The moon is laughing at me now—I can see his grin through the trees. Get to the edge of the wood, to the little bridge and across, with the river below black satin and quiet, lying in wait with shivery icy fingers to pull you in. Up the bank past the big sycamore and the ruined cottage near our home—time to catch my breath and wait for my fear to become silly again.

The door opens and out come the dogs, running to meet me. Love me they do, my dogs. Judy, soft bracken-brown with a silly face and one ear up and the other one flat, is my pillow in the fields, as I watch the deep blue summer sky high above green leaves. They rush on me, excited, and fuss me into the house, till my father calls them. 'Good girls, to bed.' Into the barn they go to sleep on sweet hay beds.

Inside now with my dad, and my mam is making sandwiches for my dad's and brother's work boxes. Slabs of fruit cake, four Welsh cakes, and big culfs of crusty bread and cheese.

'Hello Bach, and where've you been, and get the bath now, is it?' My dad opens up the stove door to see the fire grinning through the bars, and fills the frost patterned tin bath with water. Too hot, too cold, any old delaying tactics.

No shampoo, just a bar of Puritan soap, and I hope it's had its corners worn off. New bars knobble across your scalp and why can't I have Loxene like Mair Davies, my arch enemy? She has everything including a fluffy cardigan, lace-up daps, and a best dress for school photo days.

Out of the bath, glowing like a beacon, shining as apples. Into a winceyette nightie sewn by my mother in the shape of a big flat T and patterned all over with candles.

Mam is pulling my hair now into two plaits, very tight. I'm ooing and awing and nearly on the floor, trying to get away from her, but she's got a grip and I'm done. Chinese eyes on Sunday nights.

Four Welsh cakes, a glass of goat's milk and that's me, up to bed with a night light casting huge shadows, and the devil's on the wardrobe door glowing. Jump into bed quick before the hand under the bed grabs my ankle, and lie awake torturing myself, looking at the gap in the ceiling boards where a big bloodshot eye is going to look back at me any minute. Sink down into the feather mattress, get the bedclothes just right over my eyes to see nothing, but leave my mouth clear to breathe. Now I lay me down to sleep prayers then I lie listening to the scamperings coming from the loft. Soon Cwmcerrig night shift is clocking on. Last look around the bedroom to make sure I'm not being watched and I drift off to sleep to the murmur of my parents and the little river Siedi.

Dorinda McCann

The Witch of Bevan Lane

Meryl peered round the corner of the street at the old woman. She certainly looked like a witch. Grey-white hair hung straight to her shoulders, back bent in two as she leaned on her stick for support. Dark eyes sunk between wrinkled brow and prominent hooked nose gazed down the street in the direction from which the children usually came.

With fast beating heart and shaking knees, Meryl left her hiding place, a whispered, 'Go on, go on,' ringing in her ears.

What if she spoke to her? Or worse—asked her in as she had Rhian that time. Needless to say Rhian had run—too fast to stay on her feet and ended up with a grazed knee. They all agreed the witch had put a spell on her.

She didn't usually take dares. She hadn't believed the old woman was really a witch, but the closer she came to her the more she looked like the witches in old picture books.

Meryl's feet dragged as she neared the figure at the gate. She would have turned tail if it hadn't been for her friends' eyes boring into her back.

As she reached the old woman's garden she

quickened her pace and would have run past if a cracked voice hadn't said:

'Are you going past the pillar box? Too far for me, it is.' A hand like a claw proferred the letter.

Meryl took it and fled, not stopping until she reached the post box. She had a fleeting glimpse of scrawled handwriting on the envelope before dropping it through the slit.

She'd done it! Not only walked past her, but the witch had spoken to her—almost touched her!

For ages now, stories that there were witches in the valley had been circulating the school. Tales of lights in the churchyard at dead of night and sound of chanting coming from the derelict Salem chapel had reminded people of the old stories about Miss Mount. How she prowled the bushes round the tips looking for herbs to cast her spells—and some swore her cats took human form at midnight.

Meryl and her friends had taken to peering over the garden wall of her house which stood in the street behind their school and one afternoon had been rewarded by the sight of the witch shredding large leaves into a black iron pot to which she added liquid and stirred. It was evidently one of her spells and Meryl hoped she hadn't helped by handling the envelope.

She waited for Rhian and Emma to catch her up. Feeling a thrill of superiority, she wondered if they'd have gone through with it if it had been their dare.

They came panting up.

'What did she give you? What was she like?'

'A letter to post. You should see her eyes—and her hands are like claws! Those cats are definitely her familiars. The way they stare!'

Rhian and Emma shivered. 'We didn't think you'd do it. Come on, let's pay your forfeit at the sweet shop.'

Next time, thought Meryl, I'll have a really good look, try to see what's inside. She amazed herself. What am I thinking of—next time? I'm not going there again.

But incredibly, she found herself drawn to the place. She went that way to school, without sight of the bent figure. One day she stopped outside and craned to see if she could see through the front window, but the curtains remained drawn without even a glimpse of a whisker.

Was the old woman all right? She looked so ancient that anything might have happened. No milk stood outside, no newspapers poked through from the letter box.

She wondered if she should enquire next door. But what would she say? She didn't really know her. As she hesitated, the door opened a crack, then slowly the gap widened until there was just enough space for a cat's head to push through, then another and still the door inched open, until the old woman was revealed.

Meryl gaped. She looked older than ever, eyes sunk in dark sockets beneath the stick-straight hair. But she was smiling, a smile that revealed one long brown tooth that clamped on her lower lip.

'You posted my letter,' she croaked. 'What can I do for you?'

'I just wondered if you were all right,' Meryl stammered, stepping back a pace. 'I hadn't seen you.'

'*Diawch*! As well as my old bones will let me be,' said the witch. 'You're kind to enquire. Most children torment my cats or knock at the door and run away. Come in, will you?'

All the cautions she'd heard about going off with people sang in her ears and pictures of Hansel and Gretel flashed before her eyes, but she didn't seem able to help herself. Her legs went forward of their own accord.

Once inside, she could scarcely believe her eyes. The room was crammed with stuff, leaving only a narrow path through furniture to reach the fireplace where a couple of armchairs were spread with newspaper. Every surface was covered with ornaments, pictures or books. The table held pots of jam, medicine bottles, jars, biscuit tins, cups and saucers and a plate with partly eaten food. Piles of newspapers and black plastic bags, some with garments trailing from the tops, were stacked around the walls between the furniture. A rail, like the ones in dress shops, held a row of dresses and coats. And over everything hung the smell of cats!

Meryl thought of her mother's cross words that morning when she'd left her painting things out. What would she say if she saw this mess? But she couldn't tell a witch off, she thought with a grin, she'd put a spell on her.

'Sit down, sit down. It's not often I have visitors. Take the paper off the chair, *cariad*. I put it there for the cats to lie on.'

Meryl removed the paper from the chair. Spitting, the ginger cat jumped on to the arm and the black and white one leaped on to the back.

'Now Timmy, behave yourself—and you Missie. Get down, that's not the way to treat visitors.'

Meryl sat on the edge of the chair, wondering how soon she could escape. She'd told her mother she was going to Rhian's house. Had intended to, but somehow thinking about the witch had brought her here.

The coal fire crackled in the grate, the kettle

sang, a thin column of steam rising from the long, curved spout. A black pendulum clock ticked away the seconds. In spite of the turmoil of the room a feeling of peace reigned.

The witch seemed to have gone into a trance. She sat opposite Meryl and through half closed eyes gazed deep into the glowing coals.

Meryl looked at the photographs standing in the chaos of the mantelpiece. Faces from long ago looked sternly at the photographer. Most of them were a faded brown and white, some with black and white snapshots stuck between frame and glass, not a colour print to be seen. Were they pictures of her family? Where were they now? She seemed lonely—but then witches always lived alone.

A thought occurred to her. What if they were likenesses of people she'd lured to her cottage before turning them into toads or something? Perhaps those clothes were all that remained of them.

Meryl jumped up hastily, 'I must go. My mother will wonder . . .'

The witch, startled out of her trance, looked at Meryl with disappointed eyes. 'And not a drink or biscuit have I offered you. I'm forgetting my manners. Come again, *cariad*.'

Meryl breathed the fresh air. The smell of cats clung to her, was in the taste in her mouth and on her breath. She pulled a face; she wouldn't go there again, now she'd seen inside.

Good thing she hadn't had a drink, or it might have been the end of her. The place could do with a good clean.

She smiled again at the panic she'd experienced and felt a bit silly now she was outside again. How could an old lady like that spirit away all those people? But a little voice inside her reminded her that a powerful spell could do anything.

She didn't tell Rhian and Emma about her visit, it would spoil things. They'd never believe her anyway. She'd keep her secret a little longer.

Weather forecasts threatened gales that week. Meryl remembered their holiday last year when a sudden violent storm had torn a tree from the earth. Crashing, it hit the side of their caravan. She'd heard the groan as it fell, the scratching of branches as they clawed the van, whispering, threatening. She'd sat in terror until the farmer towed it away with his tractor. Now she was afraid of that unleashed power.

All week, rain and hail lashed against classroom windows, boots and wet clothes steamed in cloakrooms giving off a strange mixture of odours.

After school, the girls hunched in their coats,

hurried through darkened streets, too cold and wet for games of dare or peering round corners looking for witches and their familiars.

On Thursday afternoon, Miss Davies told Meryl to stay behind after class. She'd found caricatures of herself in Meryl's exercise book. Miss Davies taught Welsh—not Meryl's best subject—and the unflattering drawings had brought matters to a head.

'Now,' Miss Davies said, as she ticked three sets of exercises, 'to make up the time you've wasted, you will do these by tomorrow morning. If you paid as much attention to your Welsh lessons as you do to drawing, your work might improve.'

Meryl looked at her book and groaned. Her family were not Welsh, none of them spoke the language and Meryl found it difficult to learn. It just made no sense to her.

Outside, it was bitterly cold and a heavy layer of cloud hung over the town making it dark as night. The full force of the wind hit Meryl as she emerged into the playground. There were no friendly groups chatting before leaving for home, only the trees at the edge of the yard tossing and bowing in the wind. She stumbled, almost fell over a large branch lying across her path. The fear she'd experienced on holiday returned. She looked fearfully at the monsters looming above her, reaching out for her.

Pulling her coat closer about her, she tried to run, but the wind pushed against her, forcing her back. Further up the road, past the witch's house, lay a clear way, no overhanging branches, just houses and soon after that she'd be home.

Meryl wondered how the old woman managed in this rough weather. She was barely able to stand, let alone walk to the corner shop to buy food. Rhian said she ate bats and lizards, stewed up with herbs.

She forgot the old lady as a large flake of snow landed in her eye. It had begun to sleet with wet splodges that blurred her vision, so that she might have missed the black huddled figure if it hadn't been for the gap where the stone pillar once stood.

She'd noticed it was wobbly, the mortar decayed and fallen out. The gales had finished the job and it lay in ruins around the old lady. Blood oozed from a wound to her temple, she was drenched to the skin and unconscious. The wind tore at her skirts as if trying to lift her and Meryl was reminded of the reading they'd had in Assembly that morning about Elijah being borne up to heaven on the whirlwind.

For a moment Meryl hesitated, fear of the wind and what it had done almost making her take to her heels. Then she noticed the front door standing open. Miss Mount must have come out to call her cats in from the storm, only to become a victim herself.

Meryl ran next door and hammered on the door. A fat man, rubbing his eyes sleepily said, 'Yes?'

'There's been an accident. The old lady next door. Will you phone?'

'What's she done now? She shouldn't be living there. We're not safe in our beds.'

'Her wall's come down—she's unconscious!'

'What? Oh, all right. I'll ring for an ambulance.'

Meryl ran back and bent over the still form. What should she do? Hurrying into the house, she chose the warmest coat she could find on the rail and returned to place it over the crumpled figure.

The fat man joined her, pulling on a mackintosh as he did.

'I think a stone must have hit her head.'

'They're on their way. I s'pose we'd better not move her?'

'No, just keep her warm,' Meryl said, remembering her First Aid lessons.

She heard the ambulance coming down the long main road that linked the valley towns long before it turned the corner, its blue light flashing, the doppler note changing tone as it came nearer.

Lights began to stream from neighbouring houses as people stood at their front doors pulling on raincoats before venturing into the storm to investigate the commotion.

Suddenly, Meryl found her mother beside her.

'Wherever have you been? I've been worried sick. What's going on here?'

'It's the wi—Miss Mount. The wall knocked her out. I had to wait till the ambulance came.'

'Poor old soul,' her mother said, as they watched her being carried to the ambulance. 'I wonder how many of these gawpers have bothered to enquire how she's been faring.'

'I 'spect they were afraid she'd cast a spell on them,' Meryl said. 'Although I don't think she's really a witch.'

'That old story's not still going about is it? Good heavens! I thought people had more sense nowadays.'

'Why? What story?'

'I'll tell you about it when we get home. It's too cold to hang about here.'

She asked the ambulance men where the old lady was to be taken, then they went home.

As she prepared Meryl's tea, her mother told her the story.

'That nonsense started long ago. You see, Miss

Mount and her mother never believed in doctors. If they were ill they made potions with herbs.'

'And I s'pose people said they used them for spells?'

'Yes, and one day they took in an old traveller who wasn't well. Made him some herbal tea. He was probably dying on his feet anyway—but you know what people are like—said they'd given him something nasty.'

'You mean he died? But wouldn't they have to have—what d'you call it?'

'A *post mortem*? Yes, but that didn't make any difference. And when old Mother Evans, who'd been leading the gossip about them dropped dead suddenly—well! you can imagine! They would have had Miss Mount and her mother burnt at the stake or put on a ducking stool if they'd had their way.'

'So she's not a witch,' Meryl said thoughtfully. 'I wish I'd stayed that day. Although,' she said, with a mischievous grin, 'I might have had food poisoning. The state of the place! You'd think I was really tidy if you saw it.'

'After all I've told you about going off with strangers—that means little old ladies too. I'd have had forty fits if I'd known. I know she needed company, but ask me first before you do any more good deeds.'

Meryl hung her head. 'I wasn't doing a good deed,' she said. 'Rhian and Emma dared me. Just to go past her house,' she added hastily.

'Oh, big deal,' said her mother. 'Well, as long as you weren't one of those who knock on her door and run away. I hear the old soul's been plagued with them.'

'I did post a letter for her.' Meryl brightened as she remembered something in her favour, 'and I only went in when I hadn't seen her for a while. But she was all right—wanted me to stay for tea, but I got scared. I know it sounds *twp*, but all those photographs and clothes hanging out of the bags . . .' she shuddered, remembering.

'And your imagination worked overtime. Well, never mind, we'll find out if she's well enough to have visitors, then go and see her. That should scotch these rumours for good and all—as far as you're concerned anyway.'

Meryl scarcely recognised Miss Mount lying tightly cocooned in snow-white sheets. Her hair, combed away from her face, was secured with a hair clip. A large square dressing taped to her forehead hid the cut and most of the bruising. She looked like any other of the old ladies in the ward.

A wide smile split her face when she recognised Meryl.

'My guardian angel.' The cracked voice was still

the same. 'A brave girl you are—saved me from pneumonia.' She reached out a gnarled hand and took Meryl's. 'Thank you, *cariad*. But there's late you were. I called the other children, but they ran on. Don't know if they heard me or were afraid. It's a witch they say I am, you see.'

Meryl smiled sheepishly. 'Well, we did see you stirring something in that cauldron in your back garden . . .'

'What? *Diawch*! That was to kill greenfly! Rhubarb leaves are good for that.'

When Meryl explained why she was late from school, Miss Mount said, 'We spoke nothing but Welsh when I was a girl. You come and see me when I'm well again, I'll teach you. You can bring your mother and we'll have tea.'

Meryl looked inquiringly at her mother.

'We'll be glad to,' she said.

Joan Peake

The Dandelion Field

Bethan listened to her parents arguing downstairs. They were always arguing these days. Their anger filled the house, welled up the stairs towards her bedroom. It seemed to break against her in waves that were timed to a throb of pain in her head.

Bethan was not sure whether it was the raised voices or the headache which had woken her. She stretched her arms and legs out to find cool corners in the bed. She moved her head cautiously on the pillow. The pain was still there. A door slammed. Bethan kept very still, listening. A few weeks ago when the arguments first started, she had gone downstairs to ask her parents what the matter was. That had only made things worse. Her father had shouted at her to get back to bed, said it was nothing to do with her.

'But it is to do with me,' Bethan thought miserably to herself.

She would have liked a glass of water and a tablet for her head.

Bethan heard the radio blare on in the kitchen, then it was snapped off. The voices started again, to and fro, to and fro, each one louder than the last. Bethan let out her breath. She had thought that it had been the front door slamming, but they were both still there.

Her best friend Catrin at school had said it was okay if your Dad left. You just got used to it. She said her Dad took her on trips and bought her better presents for her birthday. Catrin's Dad had left last summer. He lived in town now with the woman from the supermarket. She had straggly hair which Bethan didn't like and they had a new baby. Catrin's Mam wouldn't go to the supermarket any more. If Catrin and Bethan were with her she made them stalk by without even looking in. It was embarrassing. Anyway, Bethan didn't believe she would feel all right if her Mam or Dad went away. She wanted them both to be at home. They didn't argue about people, though; they argued about money.

Did couples leave each other because of money? Bethan wondered.

She rested the back of her wrist against her forehead. Her skin was hot and clammy. She couldn't shut her ears, so she shut her eyes. Yellow stars flashed in sharp bursts. The rhythm was the same as the thump-thump of her head. The colour was too vivid, a sky that was all sun on huge fields, acres packed and swaying with dandelions.

'Wear a hat,' her mother had said that morning

as Bethan gathered together a selection of plastic bags from the cupboard. 'It's going to be baking later. You don't want sunstroke.'

Have I got it then? thought Bethan.

She'd certainly forgotten the hat and had spent the whole day bending and picking in the field behind the house, filling her bags with dandelion heads for her father to make wine. There were always so many dandelions in that field that, however many you picked, the field was always golden. She tried to think of the flower heads floating cool in assorted bowls in the slate-shelved larder. But what was the good of them now? Who'd bother to make wine each year if Dad left?

Cool thoughts wouldn't come. The back of Bethan's neck burned. She opened her eyes to escape the frazzle of hot yellow. Sun, flowers, flowers, sun, Mam's voice, Dad's voice, Mam's voice, Dad's voice. They all went round and round until she was dizzy.

Bethan put her hands over her ears and caught the faint smell of dandelion sap that her tea-time soaping had not quite removed. It made her feel queasy. She pictured the sap oozing and slimed across her fingers.

Bethan jumped out of bed and ran along the short landing to the bathroom. When she'd finished being sick, she rested her head against the smooth porcelain and swished water to clean the sink. She cupped her hands and splashed more water, cold against her face. No-one came. No-one heard her above the noise downstairs.

They don't even care about me, thought Bethan. They're selfish and I'll show them. It could be me who walks out.

Bethan held on to the bannister and moved cautiously down the stairs. Sometimes she swayed and had to stop a moment and hold on more tightly. The kitchen door was ajar and a wedge of light sliced across the dark hallway. Bethan craned forward. Her parents were no longer shouting but still arguing in tight undertones. They sat opposite each other at the table. Her father had a pen and a sheet of paper. He was jabbing his finger at it to make her mother look. Her mother had a shine of tears on her cheek. Bethan was appalled. Mam hardly ever cried.

'It's probably a note for me and she's got to give it to me when he's gone,' Bethan said to herself.

She wished she could step into the pool of light and tell them both how she felt.

Bethan eased the front door open and stepped out into the farmyard. She realised suddenly that her feet were still bare and the concrete was ridged slightly under her soles. A light breeze billowed her nightdress around her legs. It was cool against the burning of her skin. Bethan hesitated but it seemed too late to go back and dress. She was muddled but knew she didn't want to hear her parents' fierce voices again or see the way they sat so rigidly apart at the table.

Bethan moved across the yard. Theirs was not a large farm, just half a dozen fields that encircled the house and tipped in gentle slopes towards a river boundary. Bethan's Mam had been born there in the front bedroom on a February day when the whole valley was white with snow and even the digger from Penrhiw Fawr had failed to clear a way through the lanes to the hospital in town. Bethan had been born in the hospital. She loved the smallholding but not as much as her Mam did.

Bethan slipped past the stone barn and opened the gate to the lower field. The grass chilled her ankles. She shivered, although her body was so hot. She still felt rather sick and strangely light-headed despite the regular pulse of pain. For a long time she seemed to watch herself just standing in the meadow.

It must be late, thought Bethan after a while. There are no lights up at Penrhiw Fawr.

A glint gleam of laburnum laced the shadowed hedge. Bethan closed her eyes and dandelions prickled, bright gold and angry, in the blackness behind her lids. She opened her eyes again hurriedly. She waded through the slick grass towards the sound of water. Sometimes she swayed and had to stop for a moment but the soft murmur of the river drew her on. She tried to lose the aching beat of her head by concentrating on the gentle music of the water. It would be icy. Bethan imagined it splashing against the heat of her face.

When Bethan reached the river she didn't bother about the damp or the dirt but lay down on the bank and dangled her wrists into the swirl of water. She was suddenly very tired. She leant forward and smoothed her dripping hands over her cheeks. The almost full moon wavered a sheen of silver on the water and Bethan drowned her arms so deep into its restful light that the short, frilled sleeves of her nightdress were soaked through. At last she turned onto her back. From this position the grass looked longer. Its ragged spears pierced the sky all round her but the calm moon shone down straight into her face.

When she heard the voices, Bethan knew that she must have been asleep. Someone's hand rested lightly on her forehead. Her head felt better. There was just a faint background ache like the memory of pain. Although she had her eyes closed, there were no disturbing flashes of colour.

It was peaceful. Bethan recognised the voices as her parents immediately but their tone was gentle now, no longer angry. She did not bother to try to listen to the actual words for the moment. She just let the sounds wrap around her, close and comforting as a shawl.

When Bethan eventually opened her eyes, she wasn't sure how much time had passed or whether she had slept again. She was back in her own bed. She had a clean nightdress on and her Mam was sitting on a chair at her bedside.

'How are you now?' she asked as soon as she saw Bethan was awake. 'I told you not to get too much sun for the sake of those silly dandelions. You've given us quite a fright.'

Despite her scolding words, her voice was full of relief, not cross anymore.

She called out to Bethan's father who came into the room and held her mother's hand. Bethan liked to see them standing together.

'How did you know I'd gone? How did you find me?' she asked, remembering that she had thought they'd never miss her.

'You left the front door banging and the field gate swinging on its hinges. You were pretty easy to trace,' smiled her father.

'I must have been in a state to leave the field gate open,' said Bethan.

She paused.

'I don't like arguing.'

Her parents glanced at each other and her Mam sighed.

'Nor do I, *cariad*. It's my fault. Money's so tight that we may not be able to keep the farm. Your Dad's been trying to show me the figures for ages but it's been hard for me to admit we've got to leave. Still,' she brushed back a strand of Bethan's hair with a soft finger, 'people are more important than places. We'll survive.'

'We'll probably look for somewhere in town,' said her father. 'You'll like that as you get older. More things to do.'

'Hm,' said Bethan slowly.

It didn't sound too bad.

'As long as we're all together.'

'Oh, we'll be that all right,' said Mam. 'Now, I'll run you a bath. Your temperature seems to have gone down and you might fancy a bit of breakfast later. You had us worried for a while but things could have been much worse.'

Bethan listened to the splash of the bath water running. She got carefully out of bed and opened her curtains. The sun was up now but not too bright, not the sickening, vicious yellow of yesterday. Bethan had only ever lived on the farm and she knew she would miss it. She sighed.

Living in town would take some getting used to but Mam was right, things could have been much worse. She looked up towards the dandelion field. The yellow flowers had all gone. The whole bank shimmered in waves of silver seedheads. The field was filled with restful colour and a buoyant movement.

She watched as, here and there, a breeze rippled through the dandelion clocks and sent a feathered spray of seeds spinning into the air.

Julie Rainsbury

The Great Aunt From Hell

I can always tell when my Dad is having a crisis: he paces a lot and pushes his hands up through his hair so it stands up in spikes all over. And right then, he was having a crisis.

'There's nobody else, Dilys. I'm her only family!'

My Mum was looking mutinous and resigned by turns. Mutinous because she really didn't want Great Aunt Blodwen to come and stay; resigned because, as Dad said, the only family G. A. Blod has in the world is us. Trouble was, we didn't really know her very well. We've lived in Cardiff all my life, and Great Aunt Blod has lived in Cardiganshire all hers, and although we visited when we could, she never actually invited us, and was never very welcoming when we went. Kept herself to herself, did G. A. Blod, but now she was recovering from a heart thing, and needed somewhere to live while she got well.

I decided I'd do my Little Miss Sweetness bit. 'It'll be lovely to have her to stay! We can make a fuss of her, really get to know her.'

Mum glared at me, then shrugged. 'If she's got no one else, she'll have to come here, won't she,' she said.

My brother Alien (his name is Alun, but Alien

suits him better) was half-listening to his Walkman, half to us. 'Yeah. Let her come. But where's she going to sleep?'

Quite suddenly all the grown-up eyes were looking at me.

'Oh, no!' I said. 'NOT MY ROOM!' I'd only just got it looking just right: that is, I'd talked Mum out of pink ruffles and floral wallpaper and into dark blue walls and silver ceiling, and it had since been smothered with posters of MegaShout and Sonic DeathWatch. 'Can't she have the little room upstairs?'

Mum shook her head. ''Fraid not. She can't walk upstairs, and yours is the only bedroom on the ground floor, so it's your room, I'm afraid.'

We spent the next two days taking Sonic DeathWatch down and spoiling my lovely dark walls with pictures of cottage gardens and some awful macramé wall hanging Mrs Jones next door had made in her craft classes—all pink string and glass beads. Even the pink frilly curtains went back up and all my stuff was shifted upstairs and crammed into the box room (otherwise known as the Hell Hole). Alien thought this was hysterically funny so I rubbed his ears with my knuckles, until he lost his sense of humour.

On Saturday, Dad drove up to Cardigan to fetch G. A. Blod from the hospital. I was forced into my one totally dorkish dress, Alien had to put on a shirt and tie and stick his hair down, and Mum spent the whole day filling the house with cooking smells and panicking.

When Dad arrived with Great Aunt Blod in the back seat, his hair was standing on end, and he had the sort of look in his eye that he gets when he loses his wallet or dings the car. Sort of wild. Mum smoothed down her pinafore and she, Alien and I stood to attention in the hall. A white-haired, frail old figure struggled out of the car, slapping Dad's hands as he attempted to help. 'Fetch me my gadget, boy!'

'Boy' rushed to the boot and brought out one of those tripod zimmer things, like a grown up baby-walker, and my Great Aunt struggled into the house.

'Let me help you, Aunty!' Mum said, putting a welcoming arm about the frail shoulders.

'Get off me, woman. I can manage perfectly well. I'm not an invalid!' the old lady snapped.

I had a funny feeling that the next few weeks weren't going to be easy.

G. A. B. settled in the best armchair in the sitting room and accepted a cup of tea, sipping it while her eyes darted everywhere like pale blue hornets. Putting her cup down, she leaned towards the bookcase, and my spirits rose, thinking that if she liked books, perhaps she might fit into the family after all, and wouldn't need too much entertaining. But instead of selecting one, she ran her fingers across the tops of the books, feeling for dust. To make things worse, she found some. I watched Mum's face turn slowly purple.

At dinner, G. A. Blod suspiciously prodded the chicken casserole as if it might be poisoned, and refused to eat the raspberry meringue Mum had slaved over with a sniff and 'Give me a nice milk pudding any day'.

It didn't get any easier. Mum was nearly driven mad trying to cook while Blodwen stood over her criticising, propped against her zimmer frame. Dad was lucky, he could escape to his office, and Alien could apparently do nothing wrong: he was a boy, and she liked boys, even revolting ones like him.

But me—that was different. I couldn't do anything right.

On Sunday I was told I should be cooking Sunday lunch—if you ask me she'd had a lucky escape. Even the Home Ec. teacher has given up on me. On Monday I was ticked off for wearing my school tie the wrong way round, and told that my school shoes were disgustingly dirty (they were, but NOBODY wears clean shoes!) On Tuesday I was 'rude and pert'. On Wednesday she couldn't sleep because I was stamping in the room above, deliberately, to keep her awake; on Thursday I was sent from the dinner table to wash my hands—twice—because G. A. B. could think of nothing else but my fingernails. On Friday my Dad was told I didn't deserve any pocket money because I looked insolent, and so he had to slip it to me sneakily when she wasn't looking, and on Saturday—well on Saturday, everything came to a head.

Every Saturday there's a disco at the Community Centre, and for the past year I've been allowed to go to every one. My friends Kirsty and Steff come over so we can all decide what to wear and then dress up and get ready to go, which is part of the fun, then Dad drives us there and fetches us back for safety's sake.

Mum suggested that it would be better if Dad collected Kirsty and Steff at their homes instead while G. A. Blod was staying with us. So that was the first part of our Saturday fun spoiled. Then, without my friends to advise me, I couldn't decide what to wear, and had to try on everything in my wardrobe, twice. I finally settled on my black mini, my Sonic Deathwatch T-shirt, and my Doc Martens. I added a couple of ropes of beads, put in my zodiac earrings, and I was ready to go.

Downstairs, G. A. B. eyed me disapprovingly,

and I gritted my teeth, knowing she was going to say something nasty.

'Ready, Dad?' I asked, hoping I could get out the front door quickly.

'Is that girl going out looking like that?' Great Aunt Blod asked in a shocked voice. 'That skirt's so short it's indecent, the top is dreadful, and why is she wearing orthopaedic boots? Does she have a weakness in her ankles? She looks downright ugly.'

It was all too much. 'You're a horrible old woman,' I shrieked. 'Don't you know it's rude to make personal remarks?'

I knew, even as I said it that rudeness to a guest—even if I was speaking the truth and Mum and Dad knew it too—was unforgivable. And I knew the worst would happen next. It did. I was sent to bed. On Saturday. On disco night. I was so cross I couldn't even cry.

'I'm going to stay in my room until she goes!' I hissed at Mum when she sneaked up to sympathise with a cheer-me-up packet of chocolate chip cookies.

'I'm never coming down again, ever,' I mumbled, through cookie crumbs.

'You'll starve to death, then,' Mum said, unsympathetically. 'I haven't got time to traipse up and down stairs with trays of food for you with

Aunt Blodwen to look after.' She patted my hand. 'She's an old lady, sweetheart, try to put up with her. She won't be here forever. Just try until she's well enough to go home again.'

I said in a sinister voice, 'What if she NEVER GETS ANY BETTER! Suppose she stays FOR EVER!'

'Oh, don't!' Mum shuddered.

So I tried. Honestly. I was as sweet and as kind as I possible could be. I laughed 'Hahahahaha!' when she said I was 'no oil painting' and pretended she'd paid me a compliment; I fetched cushions, made cups of tea, was so good-and-kind I thought there was nothing she could find to criticise about me.

Wrong! I was too tall. I was too thin. I was too flippant. I was too sullen. I was too young to have a boyfriend (I haven't got one), and too spotty ever to catch one. But most of all my clothes were wrong. They were too short (indecent), too long (slummocky), too denim (jeans), too shapeless (T-shirts), too much freedom (my school sweater is oversized) and as for my long, straight hair—well! In Mum's place, Great Aunt Blod would make me cut it short and have a nice perm.

I tried not to hate her, honestly I did, but it was very, very hard. Dad's hair stood permanently on end, Mum was twitching visibly, and we changed the old lady's nickname from G. A. B. to the G. A. F. H.—the Great-Aunt from Hell. Only Alien was untouched, chiefly because he was a boy, and since he was usually plugged into his Walkman he couldn't hear most of what went on anyway. I used to have to knuckle him occasionally to cheer myself up.

Every afternoon, between two and four, G. A. Blod took a nap. One Saturday, after we'd had to tiptoe around shushing each other, and Dad hadn't been allowed to watch the rugby on T.V. in case it disturbed her, I was elected to take in her tea.

At four o'clock on the dot she had to be woken with it freshly made, one sugar, dash of milk in first (she KNEW which way around the tea had been poured, just by tasting it) and a buttered Welshcake (not half as good as she could make).

Carrying the little tray I knocked gently, and pushed open the door of what had once been my room, wincing at the pink frills and the powdery old lady smell of it. The white head on the pillow was still, the nasty pale blue eyes closed, and in sleep she looked almost-harmless. I put the tray down on the bedside table, but accidentally knocked down a large, flowery chocolate box.

It opened as it fell, scattering papers and photographs all over the floor. I glanced nervously at the bed, hoping she'd stay asleep until I'd picked them up and put them back again.

Mostly there were letters and pictures of olden-time people; men with Victorian handlebar moustaches, baggy white trousers and stripy blazers; family groups full of scowling crinolined ladies; and bare podgy babies. I hastily collected them, trying to be as quiet as I could, putting them carefully back in the box. One had slithered almost under the bed, and I stretched for it, turning it over as I picked it up. It was a full-length sepia photograph of a girl—not very old, probably about my own age. Her hair was dark, glossy and cut in a very short bob. She wore a silky, sleeveless dress barely long enough to cover slim knees clad in white stockings, a rope of pearls was wound twice round her long neck, the bottom loop dangling below her waist, and her shoes were strappy and high-heeled.

Her face was tilted upwards, her lips pursed and painted to an old-fashioned cupid's bow shape. Her eyebrows had been plucked out and painted back on again, giving her a surprised look, and below her left eye was a tiny heart-shaped black beauty patch. One gloved had rested on a slim hip, the other was elegantly holding a cigarette in a long holder close to her mouth. She was very pretty, but her face was still rounded and slightly babyish, and the elegant dress and elaborate make-up were obviously too old for her.

A noise from the bed startled me, and I looked guiltily up to see the familiar pale eyes.

'Nosing, eh? Prying where you shouldn't? Snooping!'

'N—no!' I stammered. 'I accidentally knocked them off the table when I put your tea down. I was trying not to wake you, not snooping, honestly.'

Guiltily, I held out the picture of the girl.

The strangest thing happened. Her face changed. She smiled! I'd never seen her smile before, and it made her face look quite different. She chuckled.

'Oh, my!' She took the picture. 'Oh, my doesn't that bring back memories!' Struggling to sit up, she gazed at the photograph. 'Dear me. What ructions that caused, to be sure.'

'Ructions!' I ventured, half afraid that speaking might remove the soft smile and turn her back into the Great-Aunt from Hell. But she had apparently forgotten all about me and was murmuring to herself.

'I cut off my hair, plucked out my eyebrows, painted my face, borrowed the frock and then went and had my photograph taken. Wasn't going to show anyone, did it just for me, to see if I could look like the posh city girls, but that fool photographer liked it and sent it off to the paper without asking me. Fool thought I'd be flattered!'

'Oh, when father saw it, wasn't there blood around the moon! And Great Aunt Harriet! When she found out, she was scandalised! Said I was a dreadful girl, quite gone to the bad, beyond repair.'

I sat back on my heels, amazed. 'This is you, Great Aunt?' I blurted, and suddenly she remembered me.

Instantly, the frown was back. 'Didn't think I was ever young, eh? Well I was, and just as pretty as you, too, so there.' She held the photograph at arm's length, cocking her head to one side to see it better, and smiled again to herself.

I couldn't resist it. 'Your Great Aunt Harriet disapproved of you, did she? Criticised the way you looked? I'll bet that made you feel really miserable, didn't it, Great Aunt Blodwen?'

The remembering smile was still there. 'Oh, I HATED her, girl, I hated her so much! Wasn't she ever young herself? Miserable, interfering old. . .'

And then she came back to who she was, and where she was, and who I was. And scowled. 'Minx' she said. 'Baggage! Cheeky young madam!' But there was a thoughtful look in the blue eyes, and a crease at the corner of her mouth that might have turned into a small smile if it tried very hard.

We get on better now, the Great-Aunt from Hell and me. Whenever she forgets and picks on me, I put one hand on my hip, pretend I have a cigarette in a long holder in the other, and arch my eyebrows at her. At first she scowls, but then she smiles, and she doesn't say anything more about the way I look.

Even though she's nearly ninety, and I'm not fifteen yet, I think we're really very alike. I think she knows it too.

I may even miss her a little when she goes home. Who knows?

Jenny Sullivan

Doing Things

Richard and Martin were prats. They had said they'd come down to muck about on the computer and listen to a few CDs. Instead they'd gone to a rugby match with their Dad. Wales versus Ireland or something, at Cardiff.

Paul was fed up. He wanted to be back in Swindon with his mates. He stood at his bedroom window. Mum and Dad were daft thinking it was good living in the country. Nothing but boring fields and woods and cows, and red-faced farmers crawling around in their four-wheel drives. He fancied driving a four-wheel drive. He'd take it up on the mountain and give it some stick. He'd show those dozy farmers how it should be done.

He held out his arms, hands clasped as if gripping a steering wheel. The bonnet of his Daihatsu was rearing up in front of him: the engine was roaring and straining as the tyres flung mud in every direction. He was doing thirty miles an hour . . . Paul leaned to the left as the vehicle slid sideways, clinging to the track, a sheer drop to one side . . . But that was daft, imagining things like that. Kids' stuff . . . he slumped back on his bed.

Downstairs, Susan was hacking away at her

violin again. Stupid sister Susan with her music and her dancing and baking for the village show.

Paul fancied girls like Lorna Davies. She was only fourteen, but she was always hanging round the bus shelter, scrounging swigs of lager, and sharing cigarettes with the lads round the back of The Ship. Gareth Jones said she went with anybody who had a car, but then—you could never tell with Gareth's stories. True or not, though, Lorna was sort of exciting, not like goody-goody Susan, all sweet sixteen and never been behind the bike sheds. Probably.

Paul hated being thirteen. He wanted to be seventeen at least. Girls like Lorna didn't look at younger boys. They fancied themselves too much. Susan didn't fancy herself at all, not in that way. She just did things: things that Mum and Dad thought all clever and wonderful and good for her.

She took after Dad. He was just the same—always rushing about doing things. Golf on Saturday, squash on Wednesday, Chamber of Trade on Thursday, sailing in the summer. And he was always nagging.

'Try some golf, try some squash, join the Scouts . . .'

Richard and Martin were Scouts. They were always swanning about in their uniforms and doing things, like making bridges out of bits of wood and old rope. It was all so naff.

Paul couldn't wait until he was old enough to drive: he would go to raves, drink in pubs and try it on with girls. Even computers were kids' stuff. Even the first-years were into P.C.s and Super Nintendo.

He rolled over and lay on his back, staring at the ceiling. Stupid sister Susan was still sawing away—practising for the Eisteddfod or something. They said he ought to have tried clog dancing. God, he would have looked a prat in all that fancy dress. Lorna would have laughed at him. It was bad enough being younger than her, without making a fool of himself. Gareth said she went for Heavy Metal types and she didn't like spots. Paul leaned up on an elbow and checked his face in the mirror. His spots weren't so bad— they came and went. By the time they went for good, Lorna would probably be so old she'd be married.

Mum was yelling up the stairs. What was he doing? Why didn't he come down and do something?

Like what? Paul asked himself.

Mum was as bad as Dad. She thought Richard and Martin were wonderful, always so busy with their homework and Scouts and rugby and music.

They played in the area schools orchestra and went to Drama Club in the Church Hall every week. Why can't you do things like that? she kept asking Paul. What was the point? They were like puppets, Richard and Martin: jumping about to please their parents and their teachers. He wasn't going to be anybody's puppet. Not even Lorna's—if he ever got a chance.

Richard was sixteen and had a girlfriend, a Guide who played fiddle in their dance group. She was doing A levels too—sciences. She said she was going to be a vet. She had red hair and freckles. Had she and Richard ever kissed? Paul doubted it. They were always too busy doing things. Richard said Lorna was bad news, and boring as well. But then he would.

Martin was the same age as Paul. He was all right, but he thought girls like Lorna were scrubbers. Martin didn't have much time for girls anyway. He thought they were silly.

Paul wished he could go into town. Perhaps if he hung about with the kids who messed around at the bus station and annoyed the drivers, he'd get to know Carla better. Gareth said it was good fun winding up the drivers. Sometimes the police came and got stroppy, but they couldn't do anything.

Paul didn't fancy Carla the way he fancied

Lorna. She was only thirteen and didn't think she was cool, like Lorna did. He and Carla had bunked off from the school sports, to a shelter in the park. He'd just got his arm around her and was wondering if she knew what French kissing was when this little kid had run up, with his Mum chasing after him. Carla got scared then. She was a bit tubby, and she always wore jeans, but she was all right—better than nothing. Lorna looked like one of those girls in 'Eastenders'—all made up and sophisticated. The girls in 'Home and Away' were naff—all pretty and sweet and good. Susan liked 'Home and Away' and 'Neighbours'.

Susan was still screeching away on the violin. She had been going on and on for an hour now. Paul turned on his front and wrapped a duvet over his ears. He was sure she did things just to show off. Everybody said how Susan was so wonderful and clever, and you could see her lapping it up: 'Look at me, super Susan.' Stupid Susan more like.

Mum called up the stairs again. He rolled over and stood up. He'd have to go down, to keep her happy. Dad would be back from his golf soon. At least Susan had stopped grinding away on that violin. He stretched, yawned and scratched his head. He brushed his hand over his hair. He liked it short like that. Mum and Dad had been horrified: they said he looked like a convict or something. They were so straight they were stupid. After tea, one of them, or Susan, would want to play Monopoly or cards or something just as boring. Catch Lorna doing that! She'd be going to a disco—having fun.

Paul clumped down the stairs in his Doc Martens, and tried to imagine Lorna getting ready, having a bath and getting dressed. She wore a tiny, stripey costume for swimming. Gareth said he'd seen her taking it off once: Paul didn't believe him. Gareth couldn't even say if Lorna had hairs round her whatsit. Susan did. They were black, like his. Paul had seen them once, when she'd sat on the sofa in that stupid, floppy tee-shirt she used as a nightie. He was kneeling by the music centre. He didn't say anything.

She was baking in the kitchen now, chatting and laughing with Mum. Paul took a can of Coke from the fridge, opened it, threw back his head to take a slug and leaned against the dresser. Why did Susan always look so happy? Gareth said Lorna reckoned it was uncool to look happy. But at least it was better than being bored and pig-sick of everything.

He went out into the yard. Dad's boat was sitting there, covered in dead leaves and bird muck. Dad had said it was time they made a start on cleaning it up, ready for summer. Paul ran a hand along the gunwhale. Streaks of white paint shone through the smeared mess. He looked around for a brush and bucket. He'd got 25 knots out of the old bus once last year, when Dad had given him the wheel. He had frightened himself then, but it was fun, come to think of it. Perhaps he'd try again in the summer, maybe get up to thirty knots. He began to scrub down the bows. Gareth said Lorna fancied men in red sports cars. Boats were for oldies.

Paul began to whistle. He imagined himself at the wheel, the spray flying, the boat plunging through the waves in the estuary. Dad had been talking about doing out the cabin—tidying it up. Paul reckoned a bigger outboard would be more fun. Perhaps he could talk him into it. He would have to get Dad down to Jenkins' boatyard. Paul knew a bit about boat engines. Dad would be impressed.

The sun was warm on Paul's back. He pulled his jumper off. The bows were beginning to come up nicely. He'd need a cloth and polish. He thought of Gareth Jones, jawing away to his mates. Prat. And Lorna, hanging around all day. Doing nothing.

Maybe that was why nothing ever got to Susan. She was always happy. She was never bored, stressed-out.

She was always doing things.

The Boy in Darkness

It's always dark down here. I've been in this dark for a long time. I think I've got my eyes open. The dark is heavy on my eyes.

I'd get used to the dark, my Da said. There's nothing to be frightened of, except the rats. The rats are only in this part of the pit. They don't go as far as where my Da works.

I always knew I'd have to come down here. There's no other jobs, my Da said. My brothers Gwilym and Dafydd work with Da. Gwilym shifts the drams that Dafydd fills with coal and my Da cuts. Gwilym is thirteen, Dafydd is eleven. Gwilym will be through this way, then I open the door for him. And all the others. That's my job. I'm a trapper. I trap air.

My first day my Ma said not to eat the bread and cheese in my snack-box until I was proper hungry because it'd be a long day, that first day. I had to be here by four o'clock in the morning and my Da took me home with him and Gwilym and Dafydd about five o'clock in the afternoon. Thirteen hours. A short day, my Da said. It was dark when I got up and it was dark when I got home.

My Da said not to open the box lid right off. Just open it enough to get your fingers in and the food out otherwise the rats will be at it, he said. I was hungry a long time that first day, but I could hear the rats squeaking and scuffling and I was afraid to open the box in case they ran over me. I drank from my water-jack though. There's worse things in the world than rats, my Da said.

Sitting here, in this hole cut from the rock, beside the brattice door, I can feel the weight of all the earth above me, pressing down. The timbers creak. They'll be talking to you, my Da said. Timbers can tell you a lot if you listen.

I sit quiet, in the middle of this web of dark. Every twitch and tremor of the dark I can feel. My eyes stare but I can't see nothing. The dark spreads from me along the tramway into the distance, and on the other side of the door.

All that weight above me is pressing on my chest. When I take a deep breath to shift the weight I start to cough. My Da coughs a lot. When my Da gobs up it's all black specks. Coal dust.

My Ma said some women say it's healthy—the air from the pit. They bring their babies with croup to breathe the hot air coming out of the upcast shaft. I don't think it's healthy, otherwise why would they need the likes of me down here, opening the doors to let the drams through and shutting them again straight away to keep the air.

If it wasn't for clean air coming from the down cast shaft no-one would be able to be down there, not even the rats. Even the candles would die out, my Da said. There's a furnace just beyond the bottom of upcast shaft. It draws the clean air through and this brutes with its tarry cloth traps the clean air. That's what I do. Trap clean air. It's ventilation, my Da said. The air going up the upcast shaft is full of foul air and dangerous gases, my Da said, not healthy at all.

There's firedamp in foul air. It's been in the seams of coal. Sometimes there's explosions.

I haven't been hurt yet.

I've got black rims round my eyes like my Da. It's not easy to wash coal dust out of your eyes.

When my Da came home from the pit he had a smell on him, an earth smell. When I told him, he laughed and said, 'Like moles and worms, *bachgen*, we're all creeping creatures burrowing away, except that worms and moles have it easy.' I've got that smell on me now I expect.

He works at the coal face, my Da. He gets so many drams to fill, only with lump coal. No-one gets paid for small coal. The more coal he can cut and the more drams he can fill the more he gets paid. When Gwilym came strong enough to work with him Da could call for more drams. Then Dafydd went with them and he does the filling. I don't like to see the way Gwilym has to work. He has to wear a harness.

There's women and girls in the pit as well as men and boys. My Ma used to work down here but the baby is about due so she stops up top. She used to work the windlass pulling drams up the slope. About 400 loads a day and weighing up to four hundredweight, my Ma said. She worked six days a week, seven o'clock till half past three in the afternoon. She was paid eight shillings. She's a short woman but with strong arms on her.

Sometimes she looks at my Da when he's washing. He had a straight back, white as milk, but since he's been working the new seam he's gone stooped. The new seam is lower than our kitchen table. My Ma doesn't say anything.

I'd like if I could have a bit of schooling. I could bring a slate to write on and a chip of slate to write with, if I could have a candle. When they get paid my Ma can write her name, my Da makes his mark. He gets paid fifteen shillings. I get fivepence a day but it's paid to Da. It's as well my Da can't read because his eyesight isn't what it was. It's working by candlelight as does it, my Ma said.

Sometimes if a collier passes me and has a spare candle-end on him he'll give me one and light it for me. The flame flickers and trembles and casts my shadow and that trembles too, but it's company while it lasts. It only pushes away the dark a little bit, but I warm my hands, and it's then I can sing. I daren't sing in the dark.

There's a noise in the dark. In the far darkness there's a rumble of iron. It's a dram coming through. Now it's close I pull the rope in my hand to open the door. I can smell the sweat on him as Gwilym crawls past me on his hands and feet pulling the dram. He is shackled to the dram. There's a leather belt around his waist and there's a chain goes between his legs to the load.

He doesn't stop long once he's though the door. There's nothing much to say. The belt and the chain rubs his skin raw.

Gwilym pulls four to five hundredweight each load, my Da said. He has to pull the loads to the winding shaft. Where does all this coal go from there? It's for the iron works, my Da said.

Open the door. Shut the door. How many times in a day I don't know. Even a day as long as a year comes to an end. Da and Gwilym and Dafydd and me go home then.

When we go home the dark outside is lit by red glare. Dross from the iron forges tipped out, it is, my Da said. It rolls down the sides of the tip. Elias Williams has got book learning and he said it's like a volcano. I don't know what is that volcano but it must be a fearful thing if it's like the Great Tip. There's a glow from the works as well. The stones on the road cast shadows by the light of the glare and we can see to go home.

Sundays, if it's not raining, we go up the mountain. It's nice up the mountain once you get past the tips. Sometimes my Da snares a rabbit and we have it for our bit of dinner. My Ma cooks it with onions and potatoes. Sundays I like, but for the thought of Mondays.

My Ma doesn't know it yet but Da's going after the Fireman's job. It'll be more money. There's been trouble over firedamp building up and stopping work. Sion Evans, the regular Fireman, isn't coming back it seems, since the blast that hurt him.

I heard my Ma and Da rowing. She knows now.

'It'll be right,' my Da said. 'I've got ideas how to do it. I'm careful,' my Da said.

'So was Sion Evans,' my Ma said.

The way Sion Evans did it was like this, my Da said. He found where the firedamp was thickest. It rises up and collects near the roof see, and he dug a hole under where it was and collected timbers over the hole to save his head. Then he put a long string around a candle and set it a distance away from the hole, then he lit the candle, got into the hole he'd dug, and pulled the flame towards him with the string. Bang! and the firedamp would be all burned up and the place would be safe for colliers to work in again.

My Da got hold of a lot of sacking cloth and asked my Ma to make him a robe with a hood on it.

'What for?' my Ma said.

'You make me that robe and I'll tell you what for,' my Da said.

She made it, then he told her. He was going after the Fireman's job whatever she said. He would soak the sacking robe in water and wear it to protect him when he fired the foul air. He'd have a long stick with a lit candle stuck on the end and he'd crouch down and push the flame to where the firedamp was. He'd fling himself flat when it exploded and the blast and fire would go over him, my Da said.

'The job's too dangerous,' my Ma said.

'Mining's dangerous,' my Da said. 'There's plenty of explosions set off accidental. This way it's done deliberate by someone who knows what he's doing.'

My Ma didn't say anything.

So my Da became Fireman. He could tell where the firedamp was because when he tested the air the candle flame would turn blue.

The first day he was Fireman my throat went dry all day. But he was pleased.

'It worked, Marged,' he said. My Ma didn't say anything.

My Da's pay is five shillings a day. He's going to get me an oil lamp, my Da said, but I haven't had it yet.

Some man came down the pit today. From up England way I heard Elias Williams tell my Da after. Never been in a pit before. Come to see how we get coal. He gave me such a look when he came through. He had a lamp.

'He's writing a report for Parliament,' Elias said.

'What about?' my Da said

'About children in the mines seemingly,' said Elias. 'Then they'll talk about it in Parliament.'

'What good's talk?' my Da said . . .

I know now that all this time I've been frightened. Frightened of my Da and Gwilym and Dafydd and me being hurt, frightened of darkness, but I never showed. I kept it all inside, tight and hard, in my stomach. The fright went from me yesterday.

Today I don't feel nothing.

My Da and Gwilym and Dafydd won't be taking me home with them any more. I won't see Mary, and Gwennie, and Ianto, and Shinkin Morgan again. The men brought them out after the explosion.

The darkness rocked with the terrible dull noise. Dust and lumps fell down off the roof. My ears felt a blow from the blast and the air was hot. It went quiet. Then there were shouts from the men.

'Are you all right?'

But there was no answer from my Da and Gwilym and Dafydd and the others. I opened the door for the men to bring them out . . .

Today there's only Ma and baby Gareth and me.

The neighbours have been in and out of our house all day helping. My Ma was like stone. She didn't say anything.

Elias Williams was the last to leave. He left just now. He put his hand on my shoulder and said 'Well, *bachgen*, you're the man of the family now.'

It was then my Ma began to cry.

Tomorrow is December 15. My birthday. I'll be eight years old . . .

'I can never forget the first unfortunate creature (of this class of child mine worker) that I met with. It was a boy of about eight years of age who looked at me as I passed through with such an expression of countenance

the most abject and idiotic—like a thing, a creeping thing—I have ever seen; an expression peculiar to children of the mines.'

So wrote a Sub-Commissioner in the First Report of the Commission of Enquiry into Children's Employment in the Mines 1842.

Parliament passed an Act later that year to forbid the employment in the mines of children under ten years of age. One Commissioner was appointed to see that the recommendations of the Act were brought into being. He visited Wales in 1845.

'Many provisions of the Act are not attended to,' he said.

Anne Ahmad

Summer Rain

It should have been raining the day of Gary Price's funeral. There was something wrong with the weather being so hot at a time like that. I wanted to remember the day for the rest of my life, but on hot days there would always be other things to think about. If it had been raining there would have been something to help remember him by.

Instead the sun beat down with the sort of angry and oppressive heat that makes you want to hide in the shade rather than be standing wearing a shirt and tie that was far too tight. I couldn't look at the hole in the ground that gaped in front of me. Even though I was at least six feet away I was frightened that I might fall in on top of the coffin that had been lowered in. Instead I ground the toe of my shoes into a crack in the dry earth. The grass was dead and dry as the bones, but even that was not enough.

Mum and Dad were there too. They had known Gary as long as I had, but somehow I felt as if it would have been better if they had not come. This was something I had to do for myself.

Kids shouldn't die, it was as simple as that. There should be some kind of guardian angel that at least makes sure you get through school. Gary shouldn't have died. It should have been me.

We had been larking about in the sea at Swansea. Not the greatest of places to go swimming but we could get there on our bikes within ten minutes. The Cork ferry had been crossing the bay and we had been watching it for a few minutes while we hung on to an air bed. It was a stupid thing to do but things had never gone wrong before. We had watched while the ship made its way from somewhere out beyond the Mumbles lighthouse and towards the docks. Before we knew it, we had drifted with the tide and the beach was looking a long way off. The beach was empty apart from a couple of men digging in the sand for lugworms.

'Don't worry,' Gary had said. 'I'll tow you in.' Gary was a stronger swimmer than me even though he was smaller, and he knew it, so I climbed onto the lilo while he first pulled then pushed it through the water. A couple of times the waves beat against us and I fell off the airbed but somehow managed to scramble back on again. The scariest moment came when a dead seagull bobbed against Gary's face and he had to stifle a scream. He gasped and gulped a bit in panic, and swallowed a good few mouthfuls of water. I had to help him hold onto the airbed for a couple of minutes while he recovered his breath.

I waved to a woman who was walking her dog on the beach and called for help but all she did was wave back and carry on. Somehow we both managed to hold on until the water was shallow enough for us to wade to the shore.

Gary collapsed in a heap when we were finally on dry land. At first I just thought he looked exhausted but then I saw how green he looked. He threw up where he was lying, almost without warning, his whole body going into a spasm when he did. And there was blood too, lots of it. I asked him if he was okay but it was as much as he could do to keep his eyes open. His mouth opened and closed but no sounds came out.

Singleton Hospital was less than half a mile away but I wasn't sure that Gary would be able to walk that far. He had started shivering so I draped some of his clothes over his shoulders, then carried him piggyback until the muscles in my legs turned so hard that I could barely make them work. All I could do was concentrate on putting one foot in front of the other, no matter how much the air burned my throat and chest. Gary would have done it for me without hesitating. I had to get him there, and he had to be all right.

Somehow we made it across the Mumbles Road

and almost to the hospital before a nurse spotted us and called for help. Within minutes Gary was hidden away in a cubicle with a doctor while I sat in the waiting room with a blanket wrapped around my shoulders, shivering with the cold. I waited for half an hour before anyone spoke to me again and when Gary's mum and dad arrived I couldn't even tell them what had happened. I knew they would blame me.

I thought he was just sick from swallowing too much sea water. We both knew the water was pretty filthy, what with the chemical and steelworks, and the sewerage that was pumped into the sea. I knew he was sick, but I didn't think he would die.

Then there was the funeral service. The vicar said how well he knew Gary, and how he had been such a cheerful boy, but Gary never went to the church. I never knew that vicars were allowed to lie.

Before long it was September and back to school. Mrs Williams our form teacher told everyone about Gary and I was relieved. She told them how I had carried him to the hospital and how we should all be proud of what I had done. I went red with embarrassment and then shame as she warned the class about getting out of depth in the sea. I had been worrying for the last two weeks about how I would break the news to everyone. At least this way they knew and wouldn't be asking questions about the empty place next to me.

The first lesson of the new school year was with Mr Hopkins. Gary said that he had a face like a chewed toffee but he didn't hold that against him. In fact he liked him a lot. I don't know if Mr Hopkins had been told about Gary but he said nothing.

'Today,' he said 'we are going to find out how much you know about Welsh history. We are going to make a list of important events from the past, and when they happened. But for a change, I'm not going to tell you about them, you are going to tell me. So somebody shout out a date, just the year will do if you don't know the exact date, tell me what happened then and why you think it's important. If anyone else thinks it should go on the list raise a hand. So who's going to start us off?'

I wasn't really listening to the suggestions being made. All I could hear was the scrape of chalk on the blackboard above the chatter and argument which gradually built up as more and more ideas came out. All I could see were black clouds rolling in from somewhere in the direction of the sea, and I thought of Gary.

He had loved history, and I almost smiled to myself when I thought about the day we had crawled through the undergrowth of one Port Talbot cemetery after another looking for the grave of one of the Merthyr rioters after we had been told the story.

We had to do a project and Gary thought a photograph of his tombstone would be the icing on the cake. It wasn't that important to photograph it, he was only doing that to outdo Cathryn Jones whose dad was something to do with the council and always managed to come up with something special for end of term displays. It would have been nice to have found it, but we never did. All we collected was a collection of cuts and scratches which remained sore for days.

'What about you, David?' I heard my name but was relieved to see that the question had been directed at David Calder on the other side of the room.

'1968.'

'What's so important about 1968?' said Mr Hopkins.

'In 1968 Gary Sobers scored six times in one over down at St Helens.'

There was laughter mixed in with the groans. 'I don't think that one's particularly popular, David,' he said as he rubbed the date out in a cloud of chalk dust. 'What we are looking for are dates that are important. Dates that we should remember.'

Silence. An embarrassing silence, but Mr Hopkins just waited. I put my hand up slowly, hoping that someone else would manage to beat me to it.

'Yes, David. Do you have a date that you think we should all remember?'

He knew, of course he knew. '16th August.'

Perhaps he didn't know. Perhaps I was wrong and he was going to laugh at me. 'This year,' I said, my voice almost squeaking with the strain of trying to get the words out.

'I don't think we should ever forget the 16th August. It's the day that Gary Price died.'

There was still silence for a moment. Nobody laughed, then Susan Bowen who sat on the next desk nodded her head and raised her hand. One by one the whole class did the same until everyone had a hand in the air.

Mr Hopkins rubbed all the other dates off the board then outside, at last, it started to rain.

Steve Lockley

Teachers' Booklet

to accompany

The Blue Man and other stories from Wales

compiled by

Christine Evans and Mairwen Jones

This 36 page A4 booklet contains teaching ideas for every story in *The Blue Man* collection. The focus is on exploring key themes of the stories and on suggesting follow-up activities for both group and individual work. Background information from the authors themselves is included where relevant, and ideas for further reading are listed.

15 photocopiable Pupil Activity Sheets are provided for busy teachers.

Available from bookshops or direct from the publishers, Pont Books, Gomer Press, Llandysul, Dyfed SA44 4BQ

ISBN 1 85902 209 X   £3.95

(please add 50p for postage and package to your remittance).

Also published by Pont Books:

Pont Books is an imprint of
Gomer Press, Llandysul